R, SCOTT

The Second Legacy
GABRIEL

Love Lane Books

GABRIEL

The Second Legacy (Legacy #1)
Copyright ©2016 RJ Scott
First Edition
Cover design by Meredith Russell
Edited by Sue Adams
Published by Love Lane Books Limited
ISBN 978-1973794677

DEDICATION

For Carly Mackenzie who created Micah "Six" Carlisle. Thank you, your description was wonderful.

For Rachel who nudges me along. For Elin who made me think, for Rebecca who makes me look good, for Meredith who made me a perfect cover for Gabriel, and for the army of proofers who polish and poke and make me smile.

And always, for my family.

CHAPTER 1

Four weeks ago

Gabriel picked up the scissors and twisted them in his hand, watching the bathroom light bouncing off the shiny silver. These were kitchen scissors, ones he'd liberated from the messy drawer neither he nor Stefan ever used. They'd been caught up in a mess of string, batteries, and three wooden spoons. The blades looked sharp enough, and as he couldn't remember ever using them, he hoped to hell they would do the job.

He drew them over his wrist, over the faint scar that was hidden under a tattoo, and thought about where he'd come from and what he'd done to survive. They'd held him down—gripped his hair and twisted it hard and held him down.

Just like the ones before.

Determined, he took the cold metal away from his wrist and looked back at the mirror. How did he do this? Gathering a handful of hair, he ran his fingers through the length of it, which generally brushed his shoulders, and held it high. Awkwardly, he began chopping at the dark length, ignoring the way it caught on his naked chest. He was making a real mess of this, but nothing would stop him now. With each slice of the blades, more of the curling dark hair he assumed he'd inherited from his father fell to the floor, and each push of his fingers through his hair returned less length to cut.

"What the hell?" Stefan asked from the door.

Gabriel stiffened. He'd known Stefan was home and he hadn't locked the bathroom door, but he hadn't wanted Stefan to find him doing this. Stefan would be angry; their clients liked Gabriel's long hair.

"Gabriel?" Stefan stood next to him and they exchanged looks in the mirror. "What happened?" He didn't seem angry, just concerned. Gabriel had learned to read all the expressions on Stefan's face.

"I just wanted a change," Gabriel rasped, then regretted talking at all as Stefan's eyes narrowed in on the bruises forming on his neck.

"Jesus, Gabe, what did you do?" Stefan touched him then, a brief press of fingers to Gabriel's arm, and it was all Gabriel could do not to move away. The flinch was enough, though, and Stefan stepped back. "This was an easy fucking job. How did you fuck it up?"

Easy for whom? Gabriel thought dully. Easy for the guy who'd had his friends over and decided Gabriel was fair game. What else could Gabriel expect? He'd been born to this.

"This is getting fucking dangerous, even for you," Stefan snapped, leaning on the wall by the sink so Gabriel couldn't fail to see him. "What did you do wrong?"

Gabriel dipped his eyes then; he didn't have an answer, and Stefan would lose his shit if he knew what Gabriel had done tonight. Because it had been Gabriel who'd said yes to it all. Or at least he thought he'd said yes; everything was hazy after the first vodka.

"You didn't go outside what I agreed you could do there," Stefan snapped abruptly, and stood away from the wall, his fists balled at his sides. "Tell me you didn't do that."

Gabriel hacked at another handful of hair, and this time he held on to it, dropping it into the sink and watching the curls float into a pile. He hadn't realized he had a red tint to his hair, but it was obvious against the white of the porcelain.

"Okay," he said evenly, "then I won't tell you." He was skating close to the edge, but perhaps Stefan punching him to the floor would render him unconscious and stop the fire in his brain.

It worked. Stefan cursed loudly and grabbed the scissors, tossing them away to clatter into the bath. Then he grabbed Gabriel by the length of hair that was left and twisted his fingers cruelly, forcing his head back.

"You fucking idiot," he said. "I hope they fucking paid."

Gabriel made a half-hearted attempt to get away, but he didn't really want to. He needed Stefan to do this, craved the anger and passion as much as taking his next breath.

"Did you agree to that shit? Did you even discuss a safe word?" Stefan asked, shaking Gabriel again. "Tell me what you did."

Gabriel closed his eyes and slumped a little in Stefan's hold. How could he safeword when he didn't even know at the time that he was being hurt?

And then there was sweetness, Stefan's voice gentling. "Fuck, Gabriel, sit the fuck down."

He let himself be moved, allowed Stefan to sit him on the closed toilet lid, then hunched over on himself. He was going to be sick, he hurt, and he needed to shave his head—had to get rid of every single length of it that someone could hold.

"Stefan?" he asked softly. "I made so much money." He reached into his pocket and pulled out all the cash he'd got on top of the direct payment. So much cash. Bags tumbled out with the money—tiny clear bags with white powder. Stefan would be so proud of him.

Stefan grabbed the baggies and the money, throwing the money on the floor then tipping the contents of the bags into the sink.

"Jesus, Gabe, are you high? You don't do drugs, you fucking moron. Did they make you inhale this shit? Is that why you look like death?"

Gabriel blinked up at Stefan. The words hung there, but they didn't connect in his head. What had happened? The men who'd paid for him. What had they done? Why couldn't he remember everything?

"All off," he murmured, gripping Stefan's hand and pressing it to his scalp. "Please."

"Gabriel—"

"Fuck you, Stefan, help me." He couldn't stop the curse, or the plea, or the need that itched under his skin. And he knew he'd crossed the line when Stefan's eyes narrowed and he gripped Gabriel's hair again, yanking his head sideways, exposing his neck. The scissors glinted in his peripheral vision in the bath.

"Did you get off with them?" Stefan growled, temper slicing the words staccato-sharp. "Did you?"

"Stef…"

They knew each other so well, their partnership based on years of a hell Gabriel was used to now. Stefan stood up and yanked Gabriel up after him, turning him to face the mirror, pulling his shorts down and sheathing himself. Gabriel was impossibly hard as Stefan pressed fingers to the bruises on his neck and fucked him from behind. He was still loose, pained, knew there had to be blood, but none of that mattered. He didn't have to think right now.

"Fucking idiot…" Stefan's words were harsh, ordering Gabriel to feel, and the itch under his skin was impossible to ignore. Gabriel lifted his hands, twisted his own nipples and watched his face in the mirror. Each of Stefan's thrusts knocked his thighs against the sink, and his cock was hard.

"I need…" he gasped when Stefan fucked him hard but not enough to get him off—it was never sufficient to get him off. Stefan always knew what he needed.

Stefan looks after me.

"I know what you need." Stefan pressed harder on his bruises with one hand, closing his hand on Gabriel's throat, the other wrapping around his cock. It fucking hurt; the grip and the mess in his head. "Take it—come on, you can do this."

When orgasm hit him, it was nothing. A job done. Perfunctory, a physical reaction to an extreme stimulus, but the fire in his nerves eased a little.

Stefan pulled out abruptly and Gabriel winced.

"Don't do it again," Stefan snapped. Then, before Gabriel could answer, he shoved him to sit on the toilet seat again, on a soft towel. Picking up the scissors, he began to cut Gabriel's hair, brushing the falling darkness off his skin. Then he helped Gabriel into the shower and washed him from head to toe.

This was the part Gabriel craved.

"Thank you," Gabriel murmured, hating the fact that he wasn't capable of looking after himself. His thoughts were returning to clarity.

"You're a fucking idiot," Stefan replied, with a smile that didn't quite reach his eyes.

There would be consequences for Gabriel losing control of the booking tonight; consequences that would last days. He'd known that, but at the time, a voice inside him had been shouting that if they hurt him, then he could feel something.

Anything.

They climbed out of the shower, Gabriel wrapping the biggest towel he could around him. Stefan disappeared out of the bathroom and was back in a few seconds.

"You got another letter," Stefan snapped, and threw it at Gabriel, where it bounced against his naked belly and fell to the floor. He didn't make a move to pick it up, not until Stefan had left. Fucking letters and the ache they caused. Stefan had opened it, the tear jagged, and Gabriel could imagine the temper that Stefan must have felt when he ripped it open. He didn't blame Stefan; who wanted Gabriel's past to intrude into what they had now?

He finally picked up the envelope and slipped quietly into his room, closing the door. He didn't lock it—last time he'd done that, Stefan had broken the door, told him a story about a time when he hadn't been able to get into a room and that it scared him. That he was thinking about Gabriel.

The letter wasn't long. They never were.

Legacy Ranch appeared at the top of the paper, in strong, determined capitals. Whoever this Kyle guy was, he had neat, considered handwriting. Gabriel scanned the letter and closed his eyes, waiting for the door to open.

And just like clockwork, Stefan pushed into the room, salve in one hand and a sandwich on a plate in the other, coffee perched precariously on the side.

"I made you some food," Stefan said, and sat on the bed, causing Gabriel to shift toward him. Gabriel didn't move away—he didn't want to upset Stefan.

"Thank you," Gabriel murmured.

"What did the letter say?"

That was normal. As if it was a test, even though Stefan had already read it. The first time Gabriel had said something wrong, Stefan had looked so damn disappointed. All he'd said was that he loved Gabriel but he didn't like a liar. He hadn't needed to say anything else, but the bruises had taken a long time to heal when he'd finished being disappointed with Gabriel.

"They have this horse, Mistry. Apparently it's still not been claimed."

"Anything else, Angel?"

Stefan's use of that nickname was a switch inside Gabriel that made him tense.

"The usual things—that they want to help me and when I'm ready they'll be there."

Stefan reached out, and Gabriel schooled his features so he didn't wince. Stefan cradled Gabriel's face, and his grip was firm.

"You know what will happen if you go back to that kind of life, my sweet, innocent Angel. You know they'll hurt you. You don't need help. You have me. I look after you."

"I know." Gabriel knew the right answers to give now. He'd once hoped that the world this Kyle guy wrote about would have a place for him, but that wasn't an option for someone like Gabriel.

"I look after you, Angel," Stefan said, and pressed the

softest of kisses to Gabriel's lips. "Now get some sleep. I canceled your two appointments for tomorrow. You need to eat your food, get your chocolate and sleep."

"Okay."

Stefan helped Gabriel get settled in the soft nest of pillows, and brushed Gabriel's short hair.

"This will grow back," he said.

Gabriel placed a hand on Stefan's arm. "They held my head, Stefan." He wanted to say more about what they'd done, but he didn't have to—Stefan wouldn't want to hear the details.

"It will grow back," Stefan repeated, then patted Gabriel's head. "'Night."

Gabriel watched Stefan leave, feeling more relaxed. He picked up the salve and rubbed it over his abused hole, then over any cuts or bruises he found, not entirely sure they would feel any effect from this stuff. Hell, at least his ass wasn't burning right now.

Even wrapped in the quilt, his body aching, the bruises stinging and his head cool, Gabriel couldn't get to sleep, tears crowding his eyes. Whatever they'd given him, he remembered seeing rainbows tonight, hundreds of them, in his head, and for a second he'd thought he could reach them.

"I like rainbows," he murmured to himself, to the pillow.

Then somehow, blessedly, he slept.

Chapter 2

Cam took another sip of his whiskey and it burned a steady path down his throat. It might be his first, but if someone didn't get him away from the trash he was listening to, he would need another.

"And then I just told them I didn't need their financing, not at eight percent over, so what do you think they did?"

Cam attempted to look interested, which involved nodding. He'd nod all night if it meant his charity, Stafford Canine Partners, had donations. Even with dull, bigoted assholes like his father's best friend, Josiah Harrold, bending his ear about nothing important. The same Josiah who would inevitably ask Cam about his marital status, then pity him for all the things that he thought Cam didn't have.

"What did they do?" he asked, because he knew the script by heart, and the part he had to play. Josiah was the head of the unwieldy, bloated Santone Corp, out of San Antonio, with offices in Dallas. What his dad saw in the asshole was beyond Cam, but he had to remain polite— after all, it was what he'd been trained to do.

"Only dropped it to seven, saved me a cool two million." Josiah chuckled as he spoke, and Cam wanted so badly to suggest that Josiah put the two million into Cam's charity.

He wisely said nothing. Josiah would donate his usual ten thousand, and that was more than enough to sponsor a support assistant for four months. His father and associated cronies were nothing if not predictable.

"That's a good deal," Cam said. "You must be so pleased." *Kill me now.*

And then the conversation changed, just as it always did.

"So, you caught yourself a filly yet, young Stafford?"

"No," Cam said. He wanted to poke Josiah in the chest and reiterate that he was gay, just as Josiah knew he was. He didn't; what would be the point? "I would never be able to find someone as perfect as your Dil," he added, knowing that was exactly the right thing to say.

Dilys and Josiah Harrold had been married for almost thirty years, both as obnoxious as each other, Dallas royalty, but at least Josiah didn't drown himself in perfume like his wife. Cam knew she was in the room because her scent had seeped into everything, and her voice was so damn loud. She brayed. Like a donkey. The scent was custom-made, as she often told people. He guessed it wasn't a combination of sickly sweet and lily stamens that he could detect. Knowing her, it had gold in it—or hell, crushed diamonds. She never did anything by halves.

"Shame your father couldn't make it down," Josiah carried on.

"He's busy, said to say hi."

Both of those things were a lie. He'd invited his parents to tonight's function, but they'd both cited a need to stay in Chicago. He had, however, got a twenty-five thousand dollar check, so that was something. He hadn't actually talked to them. They'd indicated through his dad's PA that they would be coming home for his sister's engagement party in just over a week, and then of course his father would be celebrating his sixtieth in July there at the hotel, so there was no sense in two trips all the way from Chicago.

A trip in their private jet to see their son, for an important event? Yeah, right—complete hardship.

Then he heard Josiah's tone change. "How's your seein'?" he asked.

Great. Not only had Josiah gone there, into the Cam-is-blind thing, but he was using that false tone, dripping with fake sincerity and with a palpable excitement that this time he might get the gossip on Cam's current medical status.

Cam owned his failing eyesight, but he didn't expect anyone else to. He was independent, in control, he had dreams. Yes, he could be resentful at times, but mostly he was okay and at peace with something he had no control over. Still, that didn't mean he wanted to talk about it all the time, or have it brought up as a talking point in company.

"Doing well, thank you, Josiah."

"Where's your mutt? Shouldn't she be with you all the time?"

"Gidget's in my suite," Cam answered.

His golden lab wasn't needed at his side for something like this event. And hell, Gidget would likely bite Josiah if the lab sensed Cam's impatience. Why Josiah insisted on calling Cam's seeing-eye dog a mutt, he'd never know. Possibly Josiah was trying to downplay the fact that Cam relied more and more on his furry companion, or maybe he was just a fucking asshole who needed a good bite from a happy canine.

A hand touched his arm, and he didn't need to see to

know who it was, right on cue. Micah "Six" Carlisle, bodyguard, best friend, and all-around hero, was rescuing him.

"Sir," Six said dutifully, "the Hythes are leaving."

"You'll have to excuse me," Cam said, and slipped a hand through Six's arm, allowing himself to be guided away and playing the blind card for all it was worth.

He and Six didn't need to exchange words; Six had his back, and would have seen that he was trapped with Josiah. He also didn't need to say that he needed air, just felt the rush of it as Six pushed open the side door and they stepped into the fading Dallas heat. Today had been so hot, and usually Cam loved that, but right now he was angsty and uncomfortable in his own skin.

"We're alone," Six said.

"Such an asshole," Cam muttered under his breath.

"Remember it's all for charity," Six said right next to his ear.

Cam felt the wall in front of him and turned to lean against it. Up here on the tenth-floor balcony of the Stafford Royal, he could still hear the hum of the streets below, the sound of distant sirens, the buzz of conversation behind the closed doors, and he concentrated on all of those things for a moment.

"Okay?" he asked, covering everything with that single word. He was asking who was there that he still needed to talk to, who was donating, who was leaving, who was staring at him as if he was a cripple, and Six dutifully reported everything.

"The Hythes really did leave," Six started. "Sheila looked ill—said she'd eaten shellfish at lunch. I personally think she was covering for the seven glasses of

Chardonnay she downed on an empty stomach. Josiah and Dilys are the power couple in the room—some nudging from company rivals, and I think we can get Josiah to double his donation if we mention John Hythe gave over fifty thousand. Oh, and Eddie Miller has a new girlfriend, or so he says."

Eddie was a portly guy, well into his seventies with a huge stake in a local tech company. He'd been one of the internet bubble survivors and banked millions on a regular basis. He was one of the nicer rich guys that Cam knew; not in the asshole leagues of Josiah and Cam's dad. Cam could remember him from when he used to visit the family, way before his eyesight had started to fail. Something had happened, though, between Eddie and Cam's dad, and they'd stopped being close friends a long time ago.

It was probably something to do with money.

"What do you mean, so he says?"

"She's an escort. I've seen her up on the twelfth floor on four separate occasions."

"Which one is she?"

Six categorized every non-paying guest in various ways. There were hookers, dog walkers, business colleagues, personal beauticians—he knew them all and had his finger on the pulse of the Dallas Stafford Royal.

"Blonde Twenty-Three," Six answered. "She's good. Seems really into him, and no one else has guessed. He probably paid a lot for quality."

"Good on him," Cam muttered. "Maybe I should hire someone to stand by me to stop Josiah asking questions about my sex life. I need a twink, wearing a cut off T-shirt, tight leather pants...oh, and he needs to wear makeup. That'll shake the bastard up with his *have you found a filly* shit."

"Yeah, hiring a hooker is not happening on my watch," Six said. "Ready to go back in?"

The door opened and the noise of the event tumbled out, spoiling the peace. Also, someone sounded angry.

"Ice in Dallas," the drawling Texas accent announced.

"It's a thing," a more measured voice responded. "Hey, Cam. Six."

Cam smiled then. He'd recognize that voice anywhere, he genuinely liked Riley Campbell-Hayes and his husband Jack, although they'd only met a couple of times since the two had got married. Before that, he and Riley had done some partying; things better left in the past.

"Hey," he said back.

"Evening," Six said in his rumble of a voice.

"You get this?" Jack said, clearly still in the middle of the heated debate he had going on with his husband. "Riley is organizing a charity event at a hockey game. Ice. Dallas. Does no one see the irony in this?"

Cam didn't for one minute want to pretend he liked sports. Not anymore. He could listen as much as he wanted, but the sports he'd enjoyed, hockey being one of them, were visual things for him. He'd stopped listening when he couldn't watch. He smiled anyway; Riley and Jack were there supporting his event, he'd damn sure support theirs.

"Count me in for two seats," he said, and extended his hand. Riley and Jack had arrived late, something to do with their children; Cam didn't ask. It wasn't a party where anyone could talk properly about anything serious.

The two men shook his hand in turn. They made small

talk for a while before someone's phone rang and they had to excuse themselves to talk to someone called Max. One of their children, Cam thought.

He turned to look out at the city. In the dark he couldn't see a thing—sometimes in daylight he could make out blurry shapes if he looked sideways on—but he remembered how beautiful the city was, and it was that beauty he recalled now. There was no way in hell he could handle kids himself, but even so he was confident he would be better at it than his own dad had been.

He inhaled the warm air, rolled his shoulders, then linked arms with Six.

"Let's get back in there."

The event only ran for another hour, and in that time Cam only got stuck with Josiah and Dilys on two more occasions, and managed to finagle it so Josiah did indeed double his donation after he casually let it slip how generous other donors had been. He chatted to Eddie's new girlfriend, Fiona. She was clearly well educated and had a lovely laugh. He liked her; he often assessed people by how genuine their laugh was. When she spoke about the charity, and there was not one single ounce of pity in her voice for him and his situation, he liked her even more, and he told Eddie so.

He could hear the blush in Eddie's voice—it was a thing, that soft chuckle that spoke volumes. Clearly Eddie was happy with Fiona, escort or not. That could only end badly, although Eddie was certainly rich enough to pay her to be with him for a very long time.

Only after everyone had left and the busy room was filled with the noise of staff clearing the tables, did Cam finally relax.

Gidget was ecstatic to see him when he got back to his room. She'd been his since she'd passed all her assessments, and was almost three years old now. Gidget was his eyes when he needed them, her harness marking her as a seeing eye dog. She was also the giver of a lot of affection, and right now Cam needed that.

Adam had left another voicemail, pleading with Cam to listen, saying that he hadn't meant to hurt Cam, that he'd been desperate.

Funny how Adam's voice left Cam feeling cold now, the betrayal and grief a heavy mix in his chest.

He sat on his bed and the mattress dipped as Gidget joined him, snuffling in a walking circle before finally curling next to him with a soft huff. He stroked her idly as he pressed the button for the next voicemail, a nicer message from the charity he funded asking him to visit for a photo shoot. He could do that—be the face of the foundation, him and Gidget.

Of course, the text from his sister asking if he still wanted his plus-one invitation to the engagement party was a kick in the balls. He knew she wasn't asking the question maliciously—she was flighty and girly, but she loved him, and they were as close as half siblings who had grown up in separate households could be. They shared a dad but had different moms, who hated each other, being wife one and wife two respectively.

The actual wedding was being held at home in the wealthy suburbs of Dallas, on their dad's sprawling acres, September time. Cam doubted the fact of whether he had a plus one or not would cause a huge issue for the engagement party, but he wasn't going to question her. She already had her hands full with the wedding. He loved his sister, and there was no way he was adding to her stress.

But if he didn't find someone to date between now and next week, he'd just amend the table settings himself, or at least get one of his staff to do it for him.

For a moment he imagined himself moving chairs, crockery and cutlery, and couldn't help smiling at the possible shitfest he could create.

Anyway, this was from the sister who had fallen in love and got engaged to her kind-of step-brother and hadn't told anyone about it. Only when they'd had to tell everyone what had happened had it become apparent that there had been no engagement party to be enjoyed by everyone who needed to be seen at these things. Cue family drama and the engagement party that was happening in just over a week.

He pulled himself back to thinking about the plus-one.

Yes, he texted, and added a smiley face. At least he hoped it was a smiley face—he'd sent her a poop emoji last week by mistake, or so she told him.

He'd laughed it off, but jeez, if he couldn't even manage to get an emoji right with his voice software, then he really was a lost cause. He'd definitely instructed the phone to send a smiley face; nothing in his memory told him he'd used the word shit in any way. At least she was the nicest of his siblings, although that would change when she was married, but that was another story for another day.

His sister texted him straight back, and he played the text through the phone. The mechanical sound of it, stilted, removed the personal punch of the message. She could have been laughing at his reply, or feeling pity, or hell, she could well be excited by the prospect that her big brother had a boyfriend he was bringing to the event. Who knew?

Is it Six? the mechanical voice said.

He hated that his sister had even asked if Six was his plus-one. He was thirty-one and he'd had boyfriends before—why assume he was bringing his bodyguard-slash-best-friend? He could have a boyfriend for all she knew.

So he lied, because lying made the pity he imagined go away, and it created an entirely new narrative for his life, one that could be looked on fondly and not laughed at.

You think I really loved someone who can't even walk in a straight line?

His ex's words meant nothing to him. Not when he'd been questioning why the guy had stayed with him as long as he did anyway.

No, it's not Six, he sent back.

A boyfriend? What's his name? Is it someone I know? She'd added ten smiley faces. He counted them as the mechanical voice spoke each one.

He couldn't exactly tell her that, as he'd just made the guy up. *You'll find out*, he hedged.

Ass, she replied, and he could almost imagine the teasing in her voice as if she'd said it herself.

Love you too, Sis.

Only when he'd placed the phone on the bed did it hit him.

He had a week to get someone to go with him.

Adam had turned Cam into a hermit when it came to men. He'd tried to steal from Cam, forging his signature to a deal he was brokering. Thank goodness Six had spotted that one. Problem was that Cam had fallen in love with Adam after a couple of months of wondering what the man saw in him. He'd been so perfect, attentive, good in bed. Well, okay in bed. Actually, pretty crap in bed—the kind who got off and went to sleep. But mostly he'd been fun and interesting, and there'd been no pity in the man at all. Not at first. But you see, a blind man can never truly tell intention, and Adam had been one hell of an actor.

Cam had fallen in love quickly and with the conviction that he'd found someone long-term. At the end of it, though, he'd realized he'd just been desperate for a connection. That was all. What he'd got had been a man who'd wanted his money and had been willing to fuck Cam if it meant he would sign on the dotted line for lucrative deals.

Luckily, Six had been all over that shit.

Poor blind Cam who needs someone to look after him all the time.

Maybe Cam had sabotaged the relationship with Adam. Maybe he'd known he was pushing Adam when he'd refused to lend him money, but Adam had turned out to be a complete asshole.

He'd find someone, someday. A man he could fall in love with for real. But that moment wasn't now.

Now he just needed a plus-one who knew the score. Six would hate this, but as Cam cuddled into Gidget, he thought about Eddie and his pseudo-girlfriend, and inspiration made all rational thoughts flee his head. He knew what he needed to do.

"Siri, make a note to talk to Six about the escort idea again."

Then he snorted a laugh.

That was some funny shit.

CHAPTER 3

Of course, the next day when Cam sought Six out in the security office, his idea didn't go down quite so well.

"This is the worst idea you've ever had," Six snapped. "I won't enable this."

Cam shrugged; at the end of the day, friendship or not, he paid Six to work for him. Still, he wasn't ready to pull that card yet, so he attempted to lower the stress he heard in Six's voice.

"It's not as bad as the time I nearly walked off the balcony of that Chicago penthouse," he joked.

Six cursed under his breath. "No."

"Yes."

"Cam—"

"Six, find me someone good, talented, nice looking, who can be my plus-one without questions from everyone. Someone classy."

"Cameron Clayton Malcolm Stafford, this is the worst idea you've ever had."

Cam knew he was in trouble when Six used his full name, so he changed direction. Manipulation wasn't his go-to option, but he had a few cards to play.

"Adam hurt me," he said. He was genuine in that statement. He'd liked Adam, trusted him, or rather he'd *wanted* to believe him.

"I know he did," Six said, and his tone had softened a little.

"I'm not ready to do that again," Cam added. "This is a compromise that works for everyone."

"I can't believe we're doing this."

"*We're* not doing anything—*I'm* doing this, and I can't believe we didn't think of it earlier."

"Jeez, Cam, you have money and a reputation as a good guy—any of the men who fawn all over you would be better than a fucking hooker."

"No they wouldn't, because I'd end up hurt," Cam said, and wouldn't let himself be dragged into more conversation. He'd made up his mind, and nothing Six could say would change it. Okay, so it had been a snap decision when he'd asked to meet Six in security, but the basics of it were something he'd been considering ever since the charity event.

He had to do *something*.

"I have to just accept that I'm not going to find someone who wants me for me," he began.

"Don't do this," Six warned.

But Cam forged ahead. Six was the only person in this entire world he could be honest with. "A blind gay man with money is, at the end of the day, a blank check with not much else going for him."

Six pushed at his chest. "I hate it when you say shit like that. You know you don't believe that."

"You're right; of course I don't believe it."

"You deserve so much more."

His friend was so damn loyal, never wanted anyone to think badly of Cam.

"Six, I'm out there looking and waiting, and I'm sick of being taken for a ride. One day I want what couples like Jack and Riley Campbell-Hayes have. I want to fight over ice in the desert, and kiss, and be in love, and not have someone rip me off for my money or take advantage. I'll have it one day, but right now I need someone I can rent just for the event."

Six made a weird sound that was half sigh, half curse, then he moved away from Cam to the bank of screens.

"Well, you need a reputable escort agency. I have numbers I can phone."

"No, I need someone with no ties to anything—no company, nothing."

"Brunet Seven is here again," Six said. "But me telling you that doesn't mean I think you taking a hooker to your sister's engagement party is a good thing."

"Six—"

"You know damn well your dad has people watching you, looking for evidence you can't cope. I can only put them off the trail for so long, because they report to me."

"What does that have to do with anything?"

"Jesus, Cam, what if your parents realize he's not a real boyfriend? Or hell, what if they think he is and they run background checks on him—"

"Stop. You would be the one to run those; they trust you for that."

"Oh Jesus, I'll be an accessory to the madness."

Cam had to change the subject, because Six sounded as if he was losing it. "Tell me about Brunet Seven."

"He dresses well, smart, good looking."

Cam moved closer to the screens and turned his head so he could try and see the picture. He couldn't make much out, but if Six said that Brunet Seven was there—or B7 as he shortened it in his head—then he was. The Stafford Royal was an elite boutique hotel, and Six was former Special Forces and in charge of all things security. If he said a target was there and had detailed descriptions and opinions, then that was fact.

"Sounds perfect."

"That was me saying he was smart and good looking...for a damn hooker."

Cam ignored his friend's anxiety and focused on the task at hand. "What does your spooky sixth sense tell you?" He waggled his fingers next to his head as he said that.

Six slapped one of his hands. "Stop that shit," he groused.

Micah Carlisle carried the nickname Six with pride, even though he said it held some pretty shit memories that he refused to share with Cam. He had a weird kind of sixth sense that gave him a heads-up in questionable situations.

"Couldn't resist," Cam teased. "So tell me what you think."

Six was suspiciously quiet, then he let out another noisy sigh. "He's focused, intense, not flashy, walks straight all the time, like he has a purpose. There's just this feeling I have that he's way more complicated than a hooker should be."

"I'll take it under advisement."

"Yeah, right," Six muttered with a sniff.

"How long has *the escort* been here?"

Six cursed again. "I could decide not to tell you anything else. Not like you can see where he is anyway."

"And there you are using a blind joke," Cam said with a mock sigh. "Anyway, you know damn well I'd ask reception."

"They don't know where he is; he came straight through. Hookers don't check in at the front desk—"

"Tell me."

"Fuck." There was a rush of air in the room, then the noise of something hitting the wall; sounded like a mug, from the crash of china. Hell, Six really wasn't happy about this, and Cam felt a prickle of guilt; after all, Six was there to look out for him like he had for years now.

That gave him pause. Was he being insane? Why didn't he find some other way to get a plus-one? Six was the nearest thing he had to a father-figure, given that he only ever saw his dad on holidays. Six was also Cam's best friend; the only one he trusted to have his back.

So why the hell was he doing this? He knew the answer lay somewhere in the middle of not wanting to open himself up to a potential boyfriend, even if he could find one he liked enough in the first place. He was told so many lies he could see through them just from the tone they were delivered in.

"Cam, please, I want you to think this through properly."

"Six. Help me." Cam pushed enough affection into his voice to say that he acknowledged how Six felt. And that yes, Six was more his father than his own dad was, and yes, he was his best friend. Then he added the killer blow, the single word that had had Six wrapped around Cam's little finger since Cam was twelve. "Please."

Six sat down heavily in the chair, and Cam heard it squeak and shake and roll back a little. He imagined Six's strings being cut and his legs no longer able to hold him upright.

"Brunet Seven entered room 1207 at approximately 11:23." Six's tone was tight.

Cam did some quick calculations in his head. "Who's in that room?"

"Young guy, works for a tech company, first stay I can find."

"Not one of our regulars, then."

"Nope."

There was a delicate balance in any hotel. The people who stayed on the prestigious upper floors had money, a lot of money, with each room costing eight hundred a night minimum. 1207 was one of the cheaper rooms at nine hundred, but it didn't matter what people paid for their room, every guest was important at the Stafford Royal. Some businesspeople, the staple of their luxury rooms, brought their family. A couple of regulars had dogs that went everywhere with them. A lot had partners who met them at the hotel. And some hired in escorts for sex. It wasn't Cam's job to judge a single person who stayed there.

But B7 intrigued him and worried him at the same time, and also fit the exact criteria for what he needed.

There was a healthy exchange of sex in this place, from the twenty-dollar hookers to the upper-class escorts. Somehow B7 seemed more at the upper end than the lower. Of course, Cam would have to rely on Six's detailed assessment.

"Can you describe him?"

"Hispanic ancestry, six feet, dark eyes and hair. Immaculate suit, muted color shirt, no tie, wears a chain around his neck and leather bracelets on his wrists. His shoes have a polish you could see your face in."

"Wait, you've seen his eyes and his shoes? You've been that close to him?"

Six noticed details like shiny shoes—that was what made him so good at his job.

"Of course I have," Six said, sounding affronted that Cam would question just how well he knew this hotel. "Up until four weeks ago, he had long hair in one of those man-buns. He chopped it off about a month back. Now it's short, and he has a tidy beard that isn't much of a beard at all. It used to be a lot thicker."

"Did you get anything on him?" Cam asked, and felt behind himself for the chair, sitting and waiting for more intel.

"What makes you think I checked him out?"

"Of course you did. You check them all out."

Six sighed. "Okay, so he lives in an apartment owned by one Stefan Milano. Second floor, nice area, so fucking for money must pay for him to rent that. No car registered to his name. I spoke to a couple of neighbors."

"You actually went to his place?"

Six said nothing at first, but Cam could imagine the look he was being given, one of impatience. "He's a regular here, and you know I follow up any crap in this hotel," he muttered. "Turns out our boy keeps himself to himself and doesn't involve himself in the community. Not that it causes a problem. People say he smiles and that they think he works in insurance. They've heard some shouting some days, and some banging, but nothing that seemed to be enough to warrant calling the cops."

"And anyone he answers to? A staff member? A pimp? Does he work with anyone else?"

"He shares his place with the owner of the apartment."

"A boyfriend?"

"Possibly."

"What else have you picked up?" This game intrigued him, and he wanted to know more.

"When he's at the hotel, he always uses the stairs to the third floor, then uses the elevator from there; post-appointment, he uses the elevator to the second floor and walks the rest of the way. Last week, on impulse, I tried to reach him before he got to the sidewalk, but he's focused, and it wasn't a well-thought-out maneuver on my part."

Six considered everything to the minutest detail, and would be pissed that this guy had somehow got past him.

"Do you have a name for him? Something other than Brunet Seven?"

"I'd prefer to file him as B7 for now."

"I need a name for him."

"Jesus. Okay. His name is Gabriel. That's all I got; there wasn't any mail in his box."

"You broke into his box?"

"What did you think I'd do? Anyway, I can't find much more without digging a lot deeper."

Cam knew that meant Six going to one of his old friends and taking the time to really dig around. That wasn't necessary, and he'd said so. All Cam needed was to make sure that this Gabriel was for hire and that he knew the rules.

"You're sure about this?" Six asked one final time.

Six never asked Cam more than once when he'd made a decision. In fact, Six was the only person in Cam's life who didn't fuss over him. There must be a reason for asking.

"Why?"

"This guy worries me, okay? Something about him. He's edgy and cautious, and even though he dresses well, there's more to him, and I don't like it."

Cam nodded. "I'll watch out for that."

"You don't have to do this," Six said and Cam sighed inwardly. Six never made a fuss about Cam and his ability—or inability—to do anything, but this was different.

"Please don't," he murmured, and heard the soft exhalation from Six that spoke volumes. Six had been his right-hand man since he was a kid and things had started to go wrong. He'd been a bodyguard hired in by parents who didn't want the responsibility of a kid who was going blind.

"Take this," Six said, and placed a small earpiece in his hand. Cam pushed it into his ear. "I wish you'd let me mic up the elevators."

"We discussed this. It wouldn't be right."

"Fucking hookers, using our place like a brothel," Six muttered under his breath, as if there wasn't a one hundred percent probability of Cam hearing him. Then he muttered something so low that not even Cam could hear it.

"It'll be okay."

"There's no eyes or ears on the inside of that elevator—"

"I'm mic'd up, and anyway you'll be waiting here, and you have the override codes if we need them."

"Cam—"

"I only need him for one evening for a dinner. I think I can handle booking a hooker," he said with steel in the words.

They sat in silence until the door to 1207 opened. "We have movement," Six said, and clapped a hand to his shoulder. "Showtime."

CHAPTER 4

Gabe waited for the elevator, a nice fifty in his back pocket and the satisfying hum of success in his head. That would be a new client. A potential regular, he thought. Short, tidy, clean, rich, and all he'd wanted was a blowjob. Gabe's kind of client. The client had booked for the next time he was in Dallas in a couple of months, and Gabe had texted a note to Stefan. What he liked most about the guy was that he didn't talk too much. His name was Mike, he was there on business, and he'd wanted Gabe on his knees with his hands behind his back, just using his mouth to get Mike off.

Easy stuff.

The first time someone went to hold his head post the shitfest a while back, he'd lost rhythm, but tonight there'd been no sign of the tense awareness that he'd carried with him for quite a few clients. Also, his hair wasn't exactly grippable anymore, if that was even a word. It was short and neat and gave very little for a client to hold on to.

Stefan had taken him to get it styled properly, looking out for him so he didn't look as much of an idiot as Stefan said he did. Not having the length around him, or the weight of the bun pulled up, was an odd feeling, but he was slowly getting more used to it.

The elevator arrived and he walked in, pressing the button for the third floor, and the doors closed. Getting off at the third floor and walking the rest of the way was just a matter of self-preservation. No escort worth his salt was caught too many times on hotel cameras, not if the anonymity the clients paid for was going to stay intact.

The elevator moved, but to his consternation it began to rise, going from this floor, the twelfth, to the fifteenth, which he knew was the top floor, the executive apartments. Money. He straightened and checked himself in the mirror, seeing only the tidy young urbane, slightly worn man looking back at him. His knees were a little sore, but that wasn't a new thing; if anything his knees were probably fucked anyway, given the pain he felt in them at times.

The car stopped and the doors opened, and a man stepped in—short, blond, cute, and dripping with money in his tailored pants and shirt. His hair was styled neatly, his face clean shaven and his scent fresh and not messed up with cologne. He was probably a few years older than Gabe—probably thirty or so—and without a suit jacket, his ass was nicely on show in well-fitted pants.

Possibly a future client?

Stefan's voice rang in his ears. *They come to you. You don't fucking tout for it. Clear?*

Yep, he was clear, but this guy, all preppy and toned? In a fantasy world, he'd be inclined to do him for free.

The first time, at least.

Gorgeous Guy slid his finger along the rack of elevator buttons, locating *lobby*, and pressed, but he didn't turn to talk to Gabe, who leaned back against the bar that went around the three solid walls of the elevator. He must be rich if he was coming down from the top floors, and Gabe almost handed him a card, then thought better of it when Stefan's voice rang louder than his own.

The elevator began to move, a smooth ride, the softness of carpet beneath his feet, soft piped classical music barely noticeable. The interior was mirrored glass, and it was big enough for a man to lie down, if slightly bent like a pretzel. And no, he wasn't entirely sure where that thought had come from.

He rolled his neck, heard the crack, and grimaced. He needed a hot shower before his next appointment, but he wasn't sure he'd have time.

The elevator lurched and came to a stop around halfway between levels eight and nine, a grinding, abrupt halt.

"What the fuck?" Gabriel said on a sharp exhalation. He waited for a moment, but the elevator didn't move and the blond didn't seem perturbed at all. He didn't turn to face Gabriel in the socially acceptable way two men in a situation like this might do.

"You may want to sit down," the stranger said, his tone soft and his accent less Texas south and more Dallas cultured. Still facing away, he gripped the rail and slid down the wall, making himself comfortable with his back to the polished mirrored interior and his legs outstretched. "This may take some time."

He hadn't even pressed the button to call for help, so Gabriel took it upon himself to do just that. Nothing. No instant connection to reception, or the fire service, or whoever the hell was supposed to come to their rescue.

Gabe moved closer and pressed other buttons. All the buttons. Including the emergency alarm again.

Nothing. No response, no movement of the car, no soothing voice saying that emergency services had been dispatched.

His chest tightened. He hated small spaces, and to be trapped and unable to get out...

"This happened last week," his companion said, just loud enough to get through the rising panic that was gripping Gabe. "They fixed it in twenty. Sit down."

"Jesus," Gabriel said, and leaned back against the wall, trying to get comfortable with his ass against the rail, then giving up and sliding down to sit opposite Blondie.

Hank would lock him away when they were expecting guests, back when he was a kid. Lock him in so he couldn't run and ruin the party. Lock him in and not let him out for hours...until he was needed

I can't do this. Help me. I can't stay in here.

The man thrust out his hand. "Cameron," he offered. "Cam," he amended.

Gabriel forced himself to look at his companion, the man's calm snapping his panic. What the hell was he doing talking to Gabriel?

No way was he going to talk to a perfect stranger. Stefan wouldn't be happy if Gabriel went outside the prescribed client list he managed. Also, the two of them were stuck in an elevator, none of the buttons were working, and panic was poking insistently at him.

So he settled back on the words from Stefan he could use as inspiration.

Always pull the mask down, Gabe. Never let the real you out. Because they'll take that from you again.

Cam's hand didn't waver, and finally, with Stefan's mantra in his head, Gabe shook it. He could do normal—he could *be* normal.

"Gabriel."

They shook and released, then Cam loosened his tie.

Gabriel also settled back—no point in sitting and worrying if Cam was right and they were stuck there. He pulled out his cell. There was no reception, but he typed out a quick text to Stefan in the vague hope it would somehow connect—otherwise he was going to be in a whole lot of shit when he got out of here.

"You need to be somewhere?" Cam asked, and Gabriel saw him push his dark-lensed glasses back up his nose. From the way he did that, it looked like they had a habit of slipping. Panic rose again, and he had to concentrate on the here and now, try to forget his past and focus on the moron who sat opposite him.

Why was he wearing sunglasses indoors? Only douchebags of the highest order did that. Added to which, Gabriel liked to look people in the eyes. You only had the real measure of a person if you could see the emotions that were betrayed in their eyes.

This is good. Focus on the douchebag, not on being trapped with no way out.

"An appointment," Gabriel answered, his voice steady and not betraying his panic. Cam was looking right at him and evidently expecting an answer. He couldn't exactly ignore the man—after all, a potential client was always worth working on if it wasn't so obviously an undercover cop that it meant you ended up getting arrested.

Stefan was right; the cops hated people like Gabriel.

Another one of Stefan's mantras.

"In this hotel?" Cam asked, tilting his head a little as he spoke.

Gabriel pulled himself back from silent contemplation and pasted a polite smile on his face. "Sorry?"

Cam cleared his throat and laced his fingers together in his lap. "Is your next sex, liaison, booking, or however you describe it, in this hotel or another one?"

More silence; an absolute stillness as Gabriel's mind raced with what he'd just been asked. He replayed the question, but there was nothing in that simple sentence that left him in any doubt at all about what Cam was asking.

Let me out of here. Someone help me.

He could ignore the question, and any minute now the elevator would start to move and he and Cam would go their separate ways. In fact, that was exactly what he was going to do. He pulled his knees up, wincing internally at the ache in them, not letting any of that show on his face.

But fuck if Cam didn't keep talking.

"We know the hotel is one of your regular venues for hookups," he said, unlacing his fingers and lacing them again.

Gabriel was good at reading people. He could tell when a client was going to come, knew if he was the grabbing type, knew the ones who shouted, the ones who silently orgasmed, and some he knew would cry. He read faces and body language because he had to—it kept him alive. And Cam was nervous, maybe unsure of what he was asking.

"Who the fuck are you?" Gabriel asked, his voice tight.

"Cam Stafford." Cam waved a hand at the elevator. "This is my hotel. Stafford. You know, Stafford Royal."

At that moment Gabriel should be saying he was a guest there, but if Cam was the owner of this place, then he'd know Gabriel was lying. A visitor, then—a beautician, or a masseur. Fuck, his head was empty of anything useful. So he sat quietly, not moving a muscle. The elevator would move in a bit, and he would stop it at the next floor. If Cam had called security, then Gabriel could talk his way out of things—he had specific words he knew to say.

Cam tapped a finger on his thigh. "I need to talk to you about hiring you."

He allowed some time for a reply, but Gabriel was happy sitting there working the silent treatment. Cam wasn't angry; he didn't look like he was calling Gabriel on his career choices. Suspicion coiled inside him that there was something going on here that he couldn't get a handle on.

And then Cam sighed and continued talking.

"So far, on the occasions my security manager has identified you working here, there's been no drugs, no damage to property, no unexplained noise—"

"What the hell is it you think I do?" Gabriel snapped, and as he spoke he shifted a little against the wall of the elevator. The carpet was soft, but his back was as fucked as his knees and he just wanted out of this box.

"You provide…" Cam paused, seemingly searching for exactly the right words. "A service."

"What the fuck?" Gabriel couldn't hold that burst of temper inside him. This was the most surreal thing he'd ever been in the middle of.

"As I was saying, as escorts go, you're one of the cleaner ones, or so I've been told."

"Clean?"

"Tidy, personable. A remarkably acceptable escort for hire."

"I'm not an escort. I get paid for sex," Gabriel interjected harshly. He'd never considered himself an escort. He was making money. He had sex for money. It was simple and not something he needed flowering up as being an *escort*. "I have sex and I leave—there's no fucking escorting."

Cam wrinkled his nose and nodded. "Good to know. But differences between your definition of prostitution and mine are not why we're here."

Gabriel refused to react. He knew his place, and he was happy with that place until everything was done. Then he might want something else, but not right now. This Cam guy spoke like he'd had all kinds of education that someone like Gabriel could never have accessed.

"Actually, the reason we're talking is that I want to hire you. For four hours, maybe five, and I will pay to cover any pre-existing clients you might have booked in at the time I need you."

"What?" Gabriel was bewildered by all of this, because what the hell was this asshole on?

Cam ignored his reaction and forged ahead. "Of course, you'll need to sign a non-disclosure, and the money would be cash with no audit trail. That is if you do taxes at all."

"Jesus…"

"I will cover the cost of any and all clothes you need to purchase. That includes an obscenely expensive suit; the budget for that will be pre-agreed. The first hour of the booking is to ascertain suitable cover stories and/or share information."

"What the fuck?"

Cam sighed again. He did that a lot, and it was starting to piss Gabriel off big time.

"You're not listening—"

"What the hell is going on here? Is this some kind of

sting? Are the cops waiting for me?"

"God, no, this is a genuine business transaction. How much do you charge for an hour?"

Gabriel stared at Cam for the longest time, but he didn't look away. He probably thought Gabriel was assessing how rich Cam was, or what particular limit he could push to for money. Actually Gabriel, for all his training from Stefan, hadn't had to deal with quite this situation before, and he felt lost.

I wish Stefan were here. He'd know what to do.

"Five hundred an hour," Gabriel finally said. He didn't qualify the amount with any provisos about who he had to cancel, or whether or not there was an extra percentage on top. Nope. He just laid it out there.

"Whatever we do?" Cam asked thoughtfully.

This he could do. He had hard limits and he knew them by heart. "You can't tie me up, no drugs, no pain. I'm in charge, five hundred an hour, take it or leave it, makes no difference to me."

Cam nodded. "Okay."

What? As easy as that? I should have asked for more. "Okay?"

"Yeah. The only pain will be that you need to be anywhere near my god-awful extended family."

"What?" Gabriel shuffled where he sat. "What?" he asked again.

"This isn't for sex; I need someone to pretend to like me enough to go to a family event, and for that to happen in a discreet way."

It was at moments like this that Gabriel wished he had a handy expression that would cover the shock he was feeling. Not sex. Not a night of sex, which was what he'd thought Cam meant, but…what? A night of family? Like a proper escort?

"I don't understand," he said finally, because he really fucking didn't.

"It's a business transaction," Cam said.

"For real?"

There had to be something off here. Why would Cam have looked at him and thought he was suitable to fit in with a family?

"No sex." Cam shuffled a little. "I want you to pretend we just met, you were a guest at the hotel, and the event next week is our first date. I thought that through so you wouldn't have to remember too many things about me, or what kind of relationship we'd had so far. Hell, you don't even have to know a thing about me; just that we met in an elevator."

"Sitting, eating, pretending, no sex."

"Yep."

"For five hours."

"Are you saying you can't do that?"

No, of course I can't do that.

Instead he imagined Stefan sitting there and what he would say right now. "Let's talk money," he said. Money was important.

Cam tapped his lower lip with his finger and looked thoughtful, staring off at the wall behind Gabriel. "We already did."

"But you'd be interrupting my busiest time…"

"I didn't tell you when it was."

"When is it?" Gabriel asked.

"A week from Friday."

"Yep, I'd have to turn away clients."

"And?"

"That changes things. So, two five for the evening, no sex."

"Five hundred total."

"What the hell?" Gabriel wasn't used to negotiating. "Eighteen, and that's as low as I go."

Cam didn't even flinch. He held out a hand. "I'll go to six, and that is as high as I will go."

Gabriel hesitated. He'd actually managed to get another hundred out of the man, and that was another hundred in Stefan's hands. He shook on it.

Stefan will *be proud.*

Cam was still talking, and that swell of pleasure at what Stefan would think diminished abruptly.

"I'll need you in your new and hideously expensive suit, seven p.m., a week from Friday, room 1502. My security manager will talk to you about a budget for clothes."

Gabriel entered the details into his phone and pocketed the cell. Six hundred dollars, take off what he paid Stefan, meant he'd be able to save some.

Cam tapped his ear. "You can take us down," he said.

What did Cam mean? Who was he talking to? "What are you doing?" Gabriel said.

Cam frowned and pulled his legs up to his chest. "Six?" he said again.

"Who are you talking to?"

"My security man. He's supposed to be starting up the elevator now."

"What?"

"Seems my plan has backfired," Cam murmured.

"Wait. The elevator stopping—that was planned?"

"Yes."

"Jesus, why couldn't you talk to me on the fucking street?" Anger mixed with healthy fear. This was wrong; this whole situation was wrong. He needed someone to talk him down. He needed to get out of this damn tin box.

"I don't discuss personal and private matters in public."

"Get us down, then," Gabriel ordered, aware he was letting some of his fear soak into his words.

"I'm trying." He tapped his ear again. "Six?"

"Why isn't the elevator moving?"

"I don't know. Six?" Cam said firmly.

Nothing.

Panic was swelling; Stefan was going to kill him. Gabriel pulled out his phone again and held it above his head, hoping to see bars appear. Nothing. "You don't have a signal in your elevators?" he asked.

"Our elevators are secure and private spaces," Cam said.

"Wi-Fi?"

"Nope."

Gabriel reached over Cam, pressing the same buttons as before.

"Six has control of the elevator."

Gabriel forced himself to relax. Cam sounded so sure that this situation would be fixed.

Get me the hell out.

Now.

CHAPTER 5

Just my fucking luck.

That was all Gabriel could think as he sat on the thick carpet in his most expensive suit staring at Short, Blond and Cute opposite him. This man, Cam Stafford—this weirdo who wore dark glasses—owned the hotel. Another rich fucker who was messing with Gabriel's well-ordered life.

He checked his phone again. Still no damn signal, and Stefan would blow his nut when Gabriel didn't make it to his eleven-fifteen.

Shit. Stefan will have to deal with the fallout, and I'll pay for it

But it was his fault. He was the one who'd got stuck in a stupid elevator.

Quietly there was relief mixed in with the panic; Gabriel didn't even like threesomes that much, added to which he very seldom saw a large percentage of the cash, not after Stefan's overheads. Of course, following that train of thought had him very aware that he'd just negotiated money that would have put him that much closer to the target he was aiming for.

Freedom from owing a single cent of blood money to anyone.

He banged his head against the wall, and caught Cam looking his way.

"What?" he demanded of the man who'd trapped him in this godforsaken hole of a space.

"Are you okay?" Cam asked.

"Am I okay? Jesus. I'm stuck in an elevator and I can't get over how fucking creepy it is the way you were watching me in the hotel."

Cam looked confused, and Gabriel wanted to smack the confusion right out of him. Of course, he wouldn't; Cam was a paycheck, and Gabriel was all about the money. Added to which, the guy was pretty and clean, and it wouldn't be too difficult to get it up for him if it came to it. As long as he had his mouth shut. Maybe he could gag Cam when they were fucking.

Stefan's voice was in his head. *Maybe you should stop fucking swearing and pretend to have some respect for a client. They always fall for a man on his knees who shows them respect.*

"You're a prostitute," Cam said.

Gabriel lifted his chin. Here it came, some grandstanding shit about Gabriel's place in this world.

"And?"

"Someone in your line of work could bring drugs into *my* hotel, so of course security was watching you."

Gabriel sighed. Someone wanted to call him a hooker, a prostitute, a whore, then that was okay—he was all of those things and worse. But drugs? That shit wasn't right. He didn't take drugs, not willingly anyway. And he was for sure not having anything to do with the trafficking of them. He'd lost way too many people through that kind of poison.

Just people he knew. Not friends, Gabriel didn't have friends.

With the possible exception of Stefan, who stubbornly remained in his life despite Gabriel's best tries at driving him away. The worst times were when Stefan held him so gently, cradled his face, and told him how close he was to leaving him on his own after he'd messed something up.

No, not friends, just people who drifted in and out of his life ending up dead from drugs.

"Statistically there's a correlation between sex work and drugs," Cam continued with a small shrug of his shoulders.

Jesus, the asshole sounded so dry. "I have a statistic for you," Gabriel said before he could stop himself. Before the Stefan in his head could stop him.

"Yeah?"

"Yeah, it's guaranteed that only douches wear sunglasses indoors. One hundred percent always."

Cam snorted a laugh. "I like that," he said, and slipped the offending glasses off and into the breast pocket of his suit jacket.

His eyes were an incredible icy blue framed by long, dark lashes. Add in the plump, kissable lips and he was the entire package. Clearly he'd shaved today, but his five o' clock shadow was darker than his hair. That was the only thing out of place on an otherwise perfectly put-together man. The kind Gabriel might even give a discount to if he had any control over the situation.

"Better?" Cam asked, gesturing at his face.

Gabriel stayed silent; he didn't think Cam actually wanted an answer, and Gabriel knew when to keep quiet.

Tonight couldn't get any more surreal, and the elevator was way too small a space to be trapped in. Stefan wasn't just going to be pissed, he was going to worry. Since that major fuckup four weeks back, when Gabriel had messed himself up and ended up not being able to work for ten days, the deal was you shared addresses, you fucked, you left, and then you freaking texted that you were out. He checked his phone again; there were no bars, and he couldn't get a thing out to Stefan, which meant Stefan was probably considering visiting the room where Gabriel had just left a very happy business guy on his first trip to Dallas.

He banged his head back against the wall; now the night was surreal *and* a clusterfuck of epic proportions.

He wanted to ask what the hell Cam had been thinking, trapping him in this fucking elevator, but it didn't seem Cam had been thinking at all. They sat in silence; he wasn't used to talking to clients. His mom had always said he'd done enough talking as a kid, but that particular character trait had been beaten out of him after she'd died. Every word he said now was measured, and he'd run out of the energy for small talk.

"How was tonight?" Cam asked. "Was this guy one of your regulars? Because we don't have a note that he's stayed here before."

Gabriel shot him a look of horror. The man wanted to talk about tonight?

Cam didn't back down, only focused on him steadily, and Gabe felt compelled to answer.

"No."

"No what? No you don't want to talk about it, or no he's not one of your regulars?"

"No I don't want to talk to you."

"Well, what else can we do?"

Gabriel's words spilled out before he could stop them. "Two hundred cash for the best blowjob you'll ever have."

Cam merely raised a single, perfectly sculpted eyebrow. "That seems a lot."

"It's worth it."

"How do you do it differently from any other guy I've had?"

Oh jeez, had Cam just asked me for details.

Hell if Gabriel was going to give the idiot any kind of particulars on just how quickly he could get a man off.

"I'm not talking if you're not paying," he said firmly.

Cam fell quiet for a moment, and Gabriel thought he'd stopped. Then he started up again.

"You must meet so many interesting people."

"Seriously?" Gabriel couldn't understand what the hell was going on here. He wanted to tell Cam to stop making polite conversation.

"It's what I do," Cam said. "I can be polite, I mean."

Had Cam read his mind? Gabriel shook his head. "You're not paying me to talk to you, so I'm not talking."

There. That would stop the idiot from talking and making things awkward for the booking tomorrow night. But no, Cam was reaching into his jacket and pulling out his wallet. He plucked notes from the side of it, and hell there was a lot of money in there. A couple of hundred at least. Old Gabriel would have snatched that, and for a moment he could see himself taking the wallet and running.

Running where, you idiot? You're in a freaking elevator with nowhere to run to. "How much to talk?" Cam asked.

"Fuck you," Gabriel snapped. He didn't want to talk. He didn't want to be called on his shit. He wanted things not to be so messed up right here and now.

Cam slid the notes through his fingers, rubbing them, then passed over a handful. With practiced eyes, Gabriel could see it was two hundred dollars in tens and twenties. For a split second Gabriel ignored the money, then he snatched it from Cam and shoved it in his pocket.

"That gets you ten minutes. Mouth or hand?"

A tilt of his head was the only indication that Cam had heard him. "A man uses his mouth to talk, but not, I guess, if the audience is deaf. Then you could use your hands. But I'm not deaf, so you'll need to use your mouth to answer my question."

Gabriel spluttered in an effort to come up with an answer. What was Cam Stafford taking? He narrowed his eyes at Cam, who was focused very intensely on a point beyond Gabriel's shoulder. In fact there was just something about the way he wasn't looking at Gabriel that made him suddenly wary. Was the guy on drugs? His pupils looked normal, but what if he wasn't the owner of the hotel and was instead some druggie who dressed well and would end up hurting Gabriel? Instinct had him shoving the money he'd just been given further into his pocket—no way was the asshole getting that back. He waited for this Cam guy to call him on it, but he was strangely quiet, like he hadn't even noticed what Gabriel was doing.

Fear curled inside him, but that was okay—he could handle fear, and it made his senses sharpen. Cam didn't look like a murderer, but Gabriel had seen the slickest and most expensively suited men hurt kids and adults alike.

"You're fucking mad," Gabriel said.

Cam's gaze shifted a little from the wall to him, like he'd zoned in on Gabriel's voice. "I can assure you I'm not mad. I own this place, I need a date for a family event, and you tick the boxes."

Cam was a contradiction; he owned a hotel, yet he seemed so hopelessly naïve, hiring a hooker like Gabriel for some kind of expensive event.

"So you hired a complete stranger. How do you know to trust me not to take your wallet and leave you dead in this elevator?"

Cam did his raised eyebrow thing again and shook his head a little. "You're a businessman. I am too. This is a business transaction, nothing more, and I'm worth a lot more to you than what's in my wallet right now." He didn't seem too worried about being in an elevator with an escort who might or might not be on drugs. If anything, he appeared way too relaxed after making a booking that was a third over what Stefan normally charged for Gabriel's services.

The elevator creaked a little and began to move downward, and Gabriel scrambled to stand upright, using the rail around the elevator to help him. Cam followed suit a little more slowly, and they stood in opposite corners of the elevator, looking at each other. Or rather he was looking at Cam; Cam was looking past him again. The car stopped, and Gabriel realized with horror that it was on the lobby floor. He never went down that far; preferred to stop a floor above and walk down. When you used the elevators opposite reception, they began to recognize you and any patterns you might have for return bookings. That way lay the cops if a hotel decided to get up in arms about it all.

The fact that Cam admitted security had been watching him left him cold

He reached into his pocket and pulled out a card. Cam was right, being a hooker was a business, and Stefan had got him cards because he was fucking good at his job of looking after Gabriel.

"My details," he said as the doors opened. He held out the card, but Cam didn't take it, so Gabe shook it then pressed it into Cam's hand. The man might refuse to take it, but he wasn't getting a single minute of Gabriel's time without a deposit.

"Friday," Cam said, and closed his fingers around the embossed ivory card.

Gabriel nodded and left, striding confidently through the lobby and out of the main front door. The prickle on his skin of being watched was enough to have him taking deep breaths as soon as he hit the sidewalk.

He walked away from the hotel shaken as fuck, didn't even look back, and his usual awareness of the vicinity fled. Which was how he didn't see the man until he was being guided with a tight grip on his arm into the space between the hotel and the fashion boutique next door.

That same grip pushed him against the wall, and he didn't have time to shout or yank himself away—whoever had hold of him was too strong.

His chest tightened, his breathing shallow gasps, a million flashbacks searing themselves into his brain.

He wrenched himself free and turned to face his assailant, finding himself faced with salt and pepper hair, a neat beard, and icy eyes.

"I've watched you," the man said, placing a hand around Gabriel's throat and pressing just enough for Gabriel to bring his hands up to push him away. "And you listen to me, punk. I know who you are, what you are, and you touch Cam Stafford—you even think of stealing from him or hurting him—and believe me when I say I will hunt you down and I will kill you slowly and they will never find your body. Do we understand each other?"

Gabriel tried to get his fingers under his attacker's grip, but the hold was way too tight. So he kicked into survival mode as every breath became harder to take. Then he nodded as best he could.

With one last shove, Tall, Gray and Intimidating released his hold and stepped back, then crossed his arms over his broad chest.

"My name is Six, you remember that, because I'll be watching you. Now fuck off," he snapped.

Gabriel touched his throat then let his hands drop to his sides. "Why don't you fuck off first?" he asked.

This wasn't some corner he was being thrown off. This behemoth with the short military hairstyle wasn't a cop, or anything that meant he got to manhandle Gabriel. God knew why he thought it was a good idea to confront the man, though, and he had every expectation that he would be beaten to a bloody pulp.

What the hell did it matter? He'd survived worse before.

The man shook his head in what Gabriel assumed was disbelief. "I'm watching you," he said, then turned on his heel and left.

But something inside Gabriel—some stupid, crazy bravery—had him pulling back his shoulders. "If that's the only way you can get off."

Big Man didn't even stop and turn; in fact he gave no indication that he'd even heard Gabriel, but it didn't matter. Because Gabriel had taken control of that situation. Didn't matter that the guy he'd fronted looked like a linebacker; Gabriel was never backing down to anyone again.

He headed home, walking the entire way after sending a quick text to Stefan, who responded with a code that meant he was cool, and safe himself.

Gabriel wondered idly if the threesome he had been booked for had gone ahead. If so, had Stefan got one of the others in? Had Gabriel lost the chance of a possible repeat booking?

When he got home, there was no sign of Stefan, not that he'd expected him to be there; he'd be out there wiping up the money that should have been Gabe's.

Frustrated with himself, with Cam and his booking, and with the thug who'd nearly throttled him, he stripped and walked right into his huge shower.

With the water beating down on his neck, he circled his throat with his hands, feeling the ghost of the other man's touch, and he winced inwardly, feeling sick. Coming home to his place, behind his door, with the ability and the money to run, didn't mean anything when the adrenaline subsided. He pressed hard on his throat with one hand, and the other circled his hard cock. He recalled the pain of the man's hold, the fear, and at the same time he slipped his hand up and down his cock, setting a punishing rhythm even as he tightened the grip around his throat. He knew how far he could push himself as he closed his eyes and felt the pull of orgasm.

The only way he could get off was to feel pain. Didn't matter what he'd told Cam in the elevator; pain and desperation were the only things that pushed him over the edge. His orgasm was explosive, the first one he'd had at his own hand in months; the first in a very long time.

And all because someone had treated him like shit and

forced him back against a wall.

Suddenly exhausted, he turned off the water, wrapped himself in a towel and climbed into bed, hiding away under the covers.

And he cried.

That and sex were the only things he could do really well.

CHAPTER 6

Six fifty-seven, and Cam knew Gabriel was in the building. Along with his family, all of them. His parents had their usual suite, his sister on her own in the bridal suite even though that was premature, his brothers in executive rooms, not to mention his uncle, assorted aunts, and myriad additional relatives. Getting enough free rooms at this late stage hadn't been easy but they'd managed it with overspill into the hotel next door. Added to that there was chaos in the back rooms organizing a Dallas royalty event.

All he could think was that he was so pleased the wedding itself was being held at the Stafford family home outside the city, because just one night here with all of them was enough for him to have his own private meltdown. Not to mention he had to handle his dad's sixtieth in a few months' time. More family. More drama. More fucking stress.

At least no one could pull the pity crap on him this time. He had a boyfriend now. Well, Gabriel, anyway. Much to Six's concern and obvious disgust.

Cam had spent the entire time since the elevator car telling himself he'd done exactly the right thing. He could cross one more thing off his to-do list. Book for a suit fitting, buy some more dog food for Gidget, get Six to help him find and wrap a gift for the not-very-happy couple, hire a hooker. The kind of list any man might have going on.

Didn't matter that Six wasn't talking to him, or at least

avoiding him when he could, Cam was convinced this was the only way. His dad had already made noises about taking the Stafford Royal away from Cam, and that wasn't happening. Being blind didn't make him incapable, and having a solid partner with him would prove he was as far away from abnormal as he could be.

He knew his staff, had a team he trusted, even if Six wasn't talking to him, and knew this business like the back of his hand, as befitted a kid who'd grown up in a hotel.

Stupid that he needed arm candy to prove he was able to handle it all.

But now, with only a few minutes to go, knowing that Gabriel had already picked up his deposit that morning made everything so real. Cam was apprehensive, uneasy, a sense of foreboding his friend today. His thought processes were erratic, an irrational fear that Gabriel would stand up in front of everyone and explain how poor blind Cam had to pay for a partner. His mind was going to the worst-case scenario, and he had to settle his breathing before Gidget became any more agitated.

Cam wished time would speed up so that it was past the event already, when he'd be back at work and in control of everything again. Some of the engagement party guests would stay longer, he assumed, but he could handle them by hiding away in his office.

No one expected him to be a host.

But he knew how many flower arrangements there were, had liaised with catering, organized things as mundane as table sizes, he'd done all the groundwork, and now he just had to act serene and in charge.

A knock on the door startled him, and Gidget pressed against his side.

"S'okay, girl," he reassured her. If he was going to do the big reveal, then having his service dog next to him was probably a good start.

He didn't bother asking who was at the door—no one got to this part of the hotel without Six's approval. Only Six ever visited, and he didn't knock.

Cam opened the door and stood back a little so Gabriel could come in.

"Hi," Gabriel said.

His voice sent prickles of awareness down Cam's spine. He'd never had such a visceral reaction to a voice before.

"And who are you?" Gabriel said. "Hey, gorgeous puppy," he added, and there was the noise of Gabriel fussing over Gidget. Cam opened his mouth to explain that Gidget wasn't a dog who wanted to be petted by anyone other than him and Six, but Gabriel was standing upright again.

"Can I come in?" he asked, and brushed past him, and the scent of him was familiar and as intoxicating as his voice. He sensed it when the shit hit the fan—when Gabriel evidently took a better look at Gidget and the harness Cam was holding—because he heard his sudden, shocked inhalation.

"Yes, I'm blind," he said without formality. "This is Gidget, my guide dog, and I do still have some vision in the periphery, although that will inevitably disappear. Questions?"

There was a pause, pregnant with a hundred questions. Cam had rehearsed that line so many times, having learned that it was best to take the upper hand so there were no awkward pauses or questions.

"That explains the glasses inside," Gabriel murmured. "No questions," he added, although he likely had a lot of things he wanted to ask. Didn't matter; Cam had a whole mental list of the subjects he needed to cover.

"Please help yourself to a drink." He gestured to the unit that held the brandy he liked along with other bottles he never touched.

"No thanks."

"I have bottled water in the fridge, and soft drinks. Help yourself."

"I'm okay," Gabriel said. He sounded like he was still in that confused state people often got into when they first realized Cam couldn't see them.

"Let's sit, then. We have a lot to cover in the next hour."

Cam sat in his usual place, sensing that Gabriel took the opposite sofa. Gidget settled next to Cam, leaning on his leg.

"Do you always have to wear the glasses?" Gabriel asked. "Is that, like, a blind thing?"

Cam needed them to sharpen the fuzziness as much as he could. Of course, that was getting harder and harder now, and soon he likely wouldn't bother at all. After all, no one looking into his eyes would know that he couldn't see them unless they were in his peripheral vision. His eyes were blue and normal, and Adam, despite being a lying, cheating asshole, had called them pretty. That was all he knew.

"Mostly," he answered, but didn't go any deeper. Clearing his throat, he launched into what he needed to say. "So, my sister is having an engagement party. We don't see each other much, but we do text. She's my step-sister and she's marrying my step-brother." Cam held up a hand. "I know, it's weird, but I'll explain." He gestured to the paper that sat on the coffee table between the sofas, a diagram that Six had drawn up for him.

He waited until he heard the rustle of paper, then proceeded to explain as best he could. "Ann married Sebastian and had me. Sebastian had an affair, Ann left him and married Oscar, and Ann and Oscar had Chloe, who is four years younger and my half-sister. Okay?"

"So she's your half-sister and you share a mom," Gabriel said.

"Yes. Anyway, Sebastian married the woman he'd been sleeping with, and they had two children, more half-siblings, Luke and Sophie. Luke is two years younger than me, Sophie four years. Sophie is married to a guy called Mitchell; he's an idiot, loves spending money, but Sophie seems happy, so I can't comment. None of the four of us has kids yet, so that's easy to handle. Now, this is where it gets complicated. My half-sister Chloe and my half-brother Luke are getting married in three weeks on Sebastian's estate."

"You mom's daughter and your dad's son are marrying."

"Yeah, and you understand that this is not like siblings marrying."

"Do I look stupid?" Gabriel snapped, then coughed. "Shit," he said. "I didn't mean to say see, I meant to say… jeez."

"And you can stop worrying about upsetting me with words like 'look'. You used a turn of phrase. I get that."

"Okay."

"Where was I? Right, this means that my mom has to

deal with the woman my dad cheated on her with. My mom hates the new wife, blames her for the marriage breaking up, my dad's new wife tries too hard, blah, blah. Did I mention there are no grandchildren as well? Not to forget the fact that the wedding is in September at Dad's property outside Dallas. The tension at this engagement party will be intense, but Six assures me you have signed a full non-disclosure agreement, which believe me he would enforce if anything went wrong. Also that the deposit for tonight has been paid."

"Yeah," Gabriel said, but he sounded confused, and likely not about the complicated extended Stafford family.

Cam sighed inwardly. Best to deal with the elephant in the room.

"And now to the blind thing. I began to go blind when I was twelve. It wasn't obvious at first, but it progressed quite quickly. Like I said, though, I do have some peripheral vision."

There was one of Gabriel's famous pauses, but that could be because he was nodding and would all of a sudden realize that Cam couldn't see him.

"Are you nodding at me?" Cam asked.

"Shit. No. Yes," were the three answers given in quick succession. "My bad."

"It's fine," Cam continued. "A person's voice communicates personality very effectively, before you start on about not knowing you."

"What? Where did that come from? I wasn't going to say—"

"And I don't need you to lead me around."

"Okay." Gabriel sounded almost defensive then, and Cam realized he'd laid everything out in a professional way that had likely come across as confrontational and put Gabriel on edge.

Cam wished he could see people's expressions. Gabriel had set hard limits but likely hadn't considered adding "no eating with family members" as a proviso, and now Cam was adding his own about not leading him around.

But he couldn't afford to look fragile in any way, because he was strong and determined and bucked the trend.

He thought about his dad and brother and their hotels in Chicago and San Antonio respectively. He thought of his mom, his step-mom, his half-siblings, all wrapped up in their own lives and not the most welcoming bunch. He recalled the judgments they all made about what their brother/son could handle. Then there was the extended family and their pity. He'd heard it all.

Gay? And blind? Poor Cam will never be anything more than a cripple. Have you thought about sending him away? And what if he ever does get a boyfriend? Who's to say that any man would stay with someone who can't see?

Poor Cam.

He turned slightly to his side so that he could look at the hazy image of Gabriel in his peripheral vision. Some people made the mistake of thinking he couldn't see at all, but he could make some things out if he really tried. Gabriel was facing him; that he could ascertain. His expression was less obvious, though, his face nothing but a blur. At least he hadn't turned and walked out.

"I think that's it," Cam said as cheerfully as he could. He was actually waiting for Gabriel to walk, probably with anything of value. Although he wouldn't get far—Six would lock him down before he got outside the hotel.

"What do you want me to do, to be?"

"Just be there," Cam asked, aware that was a lame answer.

"I mean, do you want me to tell people I'm in sales or something?"

"Well, I don't want you to tell them you're a hooker I pulled in for the night," he joked.

Cam heard the soft intake of breath and cursed his inability to make a joke without the stress of tonight making his words sound harsh. "I just mean tell them…" He paused. He hadn't actually thought past introducing Gabriel as his date. What if Six was wrong and Gabriel had a look about him that screamed hooker? What if he handed out business cards at the event? What if this was so fucked up that he ended up being laughed out of the room? Suddenly he felt out of control, and his fingers twitched in his lap to call for Six.

"I'll tell them I'm exploring my options, give the impression that I come from money, right? I mean, this suit is fine, and I look the part—even your psycho bodyguard thought so."

"You've seen Six."

Gabriel let out a snort, a huff of disapproval. "Seen him? He was waiting outside the hotel and escorted me up here. Didn't say a word until we got to the door."

"And?"

"He still didn't say a word. He just looked at me, and he didn't tell me to leave."

The one thing in this world that Cam believed in was his friend. It was perceptive of Gabriel to have picked up on that, and Cam didn't know why the other man's understanding of Cam and Six's complicated friendship meant so much to him.

But it did.

"What color is your suit?"

"Dark blue."

"Your shirt?"

"Pale blue. My tie is like this weird bluey-green that I didn't have much say over. Your tailor was adamant this was the right one."

Cam touched the underside of his tie just at the base, feeling the raised bump that suggested it was a red hue. He'd picked red because he wanted to be bold, and he'd pulled out his nearly black suit with a white shirt.

"Do I look okay?" he asked. He would normally ask Six, but Six had been absent, and now he knew where he'd been; sticking to Gabriel like glue.

"You want to know for real?" Gabriel asked.

"I wouldn't have said so if I didn't mean it."

"Stand up."

Gabriel stood; Cam could tell as the tone of his voice changed with the distance, and he stood too.

"Turn around."

"What?"

"I can't tell if I don't see all sides of you."

With an irritated huff, Cam turned his back to Gabriel and spread his hands. "Okay?" he asked.

Then he felt Gabriel's hands on him, skimming from the shoulders of the jacket, down his arms, tugging on one sleeve, then running fingers down over his ass and patting his thighs. The move was so quick it was barely there, but Gabriel wasn't paying lip service here—he was genuinely checking Cam was all good. And if that meant brushing his ass, and if that also meant that Cam liked the feel of the other man's hands on him, then what was he going to do about it?

"Turn back," Gabriel murmured, and Cam did as he was told.

More touches, firm, necessary, a straightening of the tie, and then he felt Gabriel move away, a quick movement of air.

"You look good," he said, with an edge in his voice.

Nervously, Cam found that bump in his tie again. Red, his tie was red.

"Yeah?"

"What else do you need me to check?" Gabriel asked, his tone a little more even. "You haven't missed any spots shaving."

"I don't—that's all done by feel. I know what to feel for." He added that last part like he had to explain, which was just stupid.

Gabriel didn't pick him up on it. "Your hair is neat, and you smell really nice."

Cam felt disappointment surge inside him. He didn't know what he'd been expecting, but he was being a needy idiot who wanted to be told more than that he was neat, good, or smelled nice. And why the hell did he want that, when Gabriel was just some street guy?

He jumped when Gabriel placed his hands on his biceps and squeezed gently. "You are a very handsome man," he said, and he wasn't being patronizing, or at least he didn't sound like he was. Then he ruined it. "Is that what you want to hear?"

All the soft-and-fuzzies that Cam had been feeling fled, and he shrugged out of Gabriel's hold. Gidget pressed into his side, likely picking up on his peak in emotion, but she didn't do her normal thing, where she moved between Cam and the person who was responsible for his anxiety.

That was the biggest thing in all this; Gidget didn't move an inch. She didn't like people in Cam's space, but somehow Gabriel had reached the same lauded position as Six.

Something about that made Cam irritable and edgy, and even rubbing his finger over the bump on his tie wasn't enough to settle him. He needed to bring this back around to business.

"No talking, right? Just stay by me, refill my drink— no alcohol, none, just water. Smile, maybe a few PDAs, enough to make this convincing."

Silence, and then the air moved and the scent of Gabriel was closer.

"What sort of affection?" Gabriel asked, way too close for comfort. Cam stumbled back, his calf knocking the occasional table, but he didn't fall, because Gabriel gripped his arm.

And he didn't let go.

Cam attempted to shake free, a small frisson of excitement running through him, but Gabriel wasn't releasing his hold.

"Do we hold hands? Kiss? Can I touch you at the base of your spine when we walk together?"

"No," Cam said, aghast. "My family is very particular about social graces. I mean a few smiles, that kind of thing. Maybe holding hands is okay."

Gabriel tutted, and he was no longer on edge from the nerves that Cam had detected when he'd first arrived. This was teasing Gabriel, this was Gabriel sliding into work mode. He still had his hands on Cam, and Cam should be scared, or at least nervous, but Gabriel's touch was experienced, secure, firm, and Cam wanted that.

Badly.

Finally he managed to shrug free—or Gabriel let him go, he didn't know which—and he straightened his jacket again, feeling the lines of the fabric against the muscles of his body. He was acutely aware of where things should lie, and everything seemed to be in place. He pressed his watch, and it told him in a soft tone that it was seven thirty-three.

"Let's go," he said. "Gidget, up."

He heard all the sounds that indicated Gidget was up on her usual spot on the sofa, and he mentally checked off the food and water that was available in the kitchen. He reached out and scruffed Gidget's fur, then walked to the door, Gabriel a few steps behind him. Right at the door, with his hand on the handle, he stopped.

"Stop them," he said. He knew what he meant. Stop his family from pitying him, stop the questions about his sexuality, his lack of a partner, the problem with his eyesight that they didn't understand and thought was terrifying. *Stop them from taking the hotel away from me.*

"I get that this is important," Gabriel said, like he'd read his mind and knew exactly what Cam meant. "Let's do this."

As soon as they reached the foyer and Cam heard the sound of his mom's voice, his chest constricted.

What the hell had he been thinking?

CHAPTER 7

Gabriel pasted a smile on his face, sickness churning in his stomach. His right knee still hurt like a bitch, but at least the pain kept him from overthinking what was happening now. He was here to do a job and he needed to do it without limping. He had to present calm, smooth, urbane, and he knew he could do it, because when Stefan had done the last straightening of his tie, he'd kissed Gabriel so tenderly and told him in no uncertain terms that Gabriel was the best out there.

The best.

But he still felt sick. Probably a combination of the heavy painkillers he'd had to take for his knee and the absolute fear that he could, and likely would, fuck this up. The money, though? That was a sizable chunk of what he'd borrowed, and the payout to Gabriel after costs taken off by Stefan could possibly put him over the next thousand in his savings account.

Who was he kidding? He knew exactly how much he had saved, to the nearest cent, and this lump sum would really help.

"Ready?" Cam asked softly.

Driven by some inner demon, Gabriel reached out and took Cam's hand, and he saw the subtle shift in Cam's expression. Fear gave way to concern, which quickly morphed into resignation. He had the most beautiful, expressive eyes, and there was no sign he was blind. The bright blue was clear, and the only thing that gave it away was the way Cam would sometimes look at him and not be entirely focused in the right place. Only ever a few inches out, but enough for Gabriel's observational skills, honed over the years by the imperative to survive, to pick up.

When Cam had opened his apartment door, right at the top floor of the hotel, Gabriel had to stop himself sighing. The man was gorgeous —his hair soft, and those eyes so damn blue, and even though he hadn't been smiling at Gabriel, he'd seemed welcoming.

All the worries that Gabriel had been feeling—from Cam being a serial killer to this being a police sting—had vanished at the soft, hesitant but welcoming smile. There had been a dimple in that smile, and Cam had looked so handsome.

Then there was the blind thing. Jeez, that had hit Gabriel from out of left field. It explained the glasses, the dog with the seeing-dog harness, and the fact that this strong, sexy man couldn't find a date without paying a whore like Gabriel.

Maybe other men didn't like his lack of sight, but Gabriel wasn't there to give a shit about what Cam could and couldn't see. He was there to pretend, and he was damn good at that. He could pretend to be dominant, he could pretend to be submissive, he could pretend to orgasm, he could pretend to give a damn about anything if it meant paying back the money he owed.

Cam glanced at him when Gabriel took his hand, and Gabriel guessed it was a reflex thing, because he wouldn't be able to see Gabriel's motivations in his expression.

"Just holding hands," Gabriel reassured him. "Come on, we need to sell this."

Cam hesitated, then momentarily gripped Gabriel's

hand before relaxing his hold again.

"Okay," he said. "Let's go."

Cam walked confidently, and after a few seconds Gabriel realized he was being led to the front desk, where a man who looked like an older version of Cam was blustering at the reception staff.

"Dad," Cam said, and stopped right by the man, who turned sharply on his heel. Sebastian Stafford; Gabriel had researched him a little. Fifty-nine, rich, head of the Stafford family since his dad had passed away at a young age in the late nineteen-nineties. He waited for Cam to introduce him, but clearly Sebastian Stafford had something on his mind.

"Cameron, did you know there were only two staff here covering the desk? Count them. One. Two."

Ouch; how was Cam supposed to count anyone? That was some insensitive shit coming from his dad. And wasn't this Cam's hotel? What right did Sebastian have to comment?

"Mr. Stafford, Julie needed a bathroom break," a petite blond explained from behind the desk.

"Thank you, Emma," Cam said firmly. "How is she feeling?"

"Better. The baby's due in seven weeks."

"Dad, let's get a drink," Cam said.

But Cam's dad wasn't letting things lie. "It's important to have an effective—"

"Not tonight, Dad," Cam said under his breath. "I'd like to introduce Gabriel Reyes."

Gabriel held out his right hand, thanking the heavens he could still hold Cam's hand with his left. He needed the reassurance, faced with an older version of Cam who stared at him like he was something you'd step in on the sidewalk.

"Sir," Gabriel said, firmly, clearly, and with a strong handshake.

Gabriel waited for the inevitable questions, but a woman stalked up to them and air-kissed either side of Cam's face.

"Cam, darling," she said. "It's Philippa," she added in a louder tone.

"Hello," Cam said dryly.

"And who is this lovely young man?" Philippa gushed, pressing a hand to Gabriel's chest. Gabriel tried not to wince at the touch. She looked like something out of a soap opera, all makeup and up-do and in a dress dripping with diamanté, or maybe even diamonds—who knew how rich she was?

"This is Gabriel, my date."

"Hello, Gabriel," she purred, and patted his chest. "I'm Cam's mother," she added.

"Step-mom," Cam corrected tightly.

Philippa giggled. Yep. Properly giggled, and leaned back on Sebastian, who was looking sharply at Cam. Thank god Cam couldn't see that look, because if looks could kill...

"Oh, you," she trilled, but there was a sharp edge to the teasing tone.

"Let's go into the room," Cam said, cutting conversation dead. He gripped Gabriel's hand tight and turned back the way they'd come, stopping momentarily before striding purposefully toward a sign that indicated this was the Stafford ballroom.

"Sorry," he muttered under his voice, but he didn't let

go. Seemed both he and Gabriel needed that reassuring connection.

The door opened, and it was a riot of gold and navy blue—the Stafford colors if the rest of the hotel was anything to go by. Balloons in displays, and a ceiling of floating balloons with fluttering tails of gold that shimmered in the light. There were ten tables, and Gabriel counted there would be eight to each table. There were pictures around the room of a couple in various poses, some professional, some candid, and the blue and gold changed in color to white as it reached the tables. Engagement party banners were everywhere, and there was a wide space to one side that Gabriel assumed was a dance floor, given the decks to one side.

Eighty sitting to eat.

"Chloe approved in principle," Cam said, and made a gesture at the wide room. Gabriel had never seen anything so celebratory before.

"Can we add in two more seats?" his dad said, not commenting on the layout or the decorations around the room and on each table.

"My friend Marcia has flown in," Philippa said, and leaned into Gabriel a little.

Gabriel moved away, bumping Cam, and it was his turn to apologize. The woman was openly leaning on him right in front of her husband, and Gabriel didn't like it.

"Was Marcia on Chloe's invitation list?" Cam asked carefully, which made Gabriel think it likely she wasn't.

"Oh no, but Luke won't mind. After all, I am mother of the bridegroom, and my wonderful son won't tell me I can't have my closest friend here."

"Of course," Cam said patiently. He gestured, and

from the side of the room someone approached. "Please organize another two seats—"

"As close to the table with the happy couple as possible, of course," Philippa interrupted, her tone less trilling and more demanding.

"See what you can do, Zachary," Cam said, with a nod to the young man who was hovering.

"Sir," Zachary said, and vanished through doors at the far end of the room.

"We'll see you here in half an hour," Sebastian said. He left with Philippa tripping after him, and then it was just Gabriel and Cam in the big room.

"What does it look like?" Cam asked quietly, and pulled his hand free of Gabriel's. Weird how much Gabriel hated the loss of contact.

"Balloons thick on the ceiling, some more around the edges...it's very blue and gold."

"And the table decorations?"

"Blue and gold. I'm sensing a theme. Your stepmom is—"

"Discussing my family is not in your remit."

Point taken, Gabriel stayed quiet and waited for Cam to say something else. He had to wait a while. There didn't seem to be an ounce of smile in Cam at that moment, and it was made worse when Six joined them in the ballroom.

"Guests are collecting in the bar," he said. "Your mom is holding court with Chloe, right across from Philippa, who has her talons in Luke. It's like a Mexican standoff in there."

"Thank you, Six, I'll go in there now."

"Any issues?" Six asked, looking briefly at Gabriel but talking to Cam. From his look, Gabriel guessed that question was about him, unless he was being paranoid.

"Nothing I can't handle," Cam said, and didn't elaborate. The lack of speech between these two was just plain weird.

Drawing back his shoulders, Cam exhaled noisily and reached for Gabriel's hand. "Let's do this."

Six looked pointedly at their joined hands, then up at Gabriel's face, his eyes narrowing. There was a warning in his expression, and Gabriel recalled the feel of the man's hands gripping his throat. He was so not going up against him—not with the danger in his face and the lethal strength in his hands. Still, that didn't stop him pushing things a little further.

The wink was very deliberate and slow, and Six's lips thinned.

Part of Gabriel wished the big, silent man would wink back—that might relax a little of the tension whirling around them.

And then Six did something that changed everything from harmless winking to something more. He held up his hand and shaped his fingers into a gun, pointing it right at Gabriel.

The message was clear.

Gabriel allowed himself to be led away by an oblivious Cam, Six close behind making Gabriel feel like death was following them.

And then everything got so much worse.

The door into the bar was wide enough that he could walk in at Cam's side, but he wished he hadn't, because the sea of faces were all looking right at him and Cam. There was a wall of sound, but it all stopped when Cam walked in. Gabriel felt like an exhibit in a zoo, but he pasted a smile on his face and didn't do what he wanted to do, which was turn and run. Cam smoothly walked straight into the crowd. This was it.

A beautiful older woman approached Cam and pulled him into a close hug, which he returned. Gabriel caught a smile on his face and the whispered "Mom". She pulled back and cradled his face.

"Sweetheart," she murmured. "Are you okay?"

She didn't wait for an answer, pressing a kiss to his cheek and wiping away the gloss that she left there.

"How are you?" Cam asked. Really formally, like they were just acquaintances. Hell, Gabriel was utterly convinced that if this were *his* mom, he'd be all over her. Moms and kids loved each other.

"Hey, big brother." A younger version of the mother cradling Gabriel's face approached.

"Hey, Chloe," Cam said, and pulled her into an affectionate hug. Now *there* was warmth and love.

"And who is this?" Cam's mom asked, and Gabriel realized she was asking about him.

"Gabriel," he said, and extended his hand.

"Anne, Cam's mom," Anne said, and shook his hand warmly.

"And I'm Chloe, Cam's sister," Chloe said with a genuine smile.

"Really nice to meet you both," Gabriel said.

He could do manners. Stefan had given him all kinds of pointers. Also, he'd mentioned that moms needed sex as well, and even though Gabriel was there for the men, Stefan always said he'd pick up the slack with any of the moms or sisters. Somehow that always made Gabriel feel slightly sick. He imagined that if he had a sister or a mom, he would want to protect them and not have them visiting guys like Stefan for sex.

"...through the hotel," Cam was saying, and nudged Gabriel with his elbow.

"Sorry?" Gabriel said, coming back to the conversation.

Always give the client one hundred and ten percent of your focus.

"Mom asked how we met; I was telling her about you coming to the hotel."

"Yes, that's how we met," Gabriel agreed, and slipped his hand into Cam's. "Our eyes met across a crowded room," he embellished.

Anne looked confused. "Cam said you were booking a conference here."

Gabriel had to think on his feet. "I know, but that sounds so boring," he teased.

Anne nodded and smiled, and it seemed that Gabriel had skirted that particular *faux pas.*

A waiter arrived at Cam's side and whispered something, and in turn Cam looked over toward a man who looked like he'd rather be anywhere than being gripped hard by a widely smiling Philippa. That must be the prospective groom, Luke.

Luke disentangled himself and came over to Chloe's side, and they hugged briefly.

"Ready?" Luke asked.

"Let's go," Chloe said.

The waiter opened the large doors, and Chloe and her fiancé had their first look at the ballroom decorated for their engagement party.

Her inhalation of wonder was exactly what Gabriel

had wanted to do when he'd seen the room; it really was pretty spectacular, and even better from this entrance spot, because the first thing your eyes went to was a raised dais dripping with flowers, where he guessed the future bride and groom would be sitting. Cam smiled broadly at hearing his sister's pleasure, and Gabriel could read the man's happiness that what he'd done for his sister had worked.

Had Cam been nervous?

Gabriel went through a few versions of his origin story. At first it was that they'd met recently through the hotel, with no embellishment, and most people were happy with that. Then it got more serious and Gabriel had to think on his feet. Turned out going back to his own real story and embellishing it sparingly was enough to make him sound authentic. No, his parents were both dead. Yes, that was terribly sad. No, he'd moved away from home a long time ago. Yes, he had a touch of Latino heritage. Yes, he'd been born near Laredo. Yes, he worked in sales.

All that was true. Even the sales part. He just assumed that everyone would react a little differently if they realized what he was selling was his body.

Finally he'd covered everyone in the entire state of Texas, or at least so it seemed.

The last couple they'd talked to, some loudmouthed, big-hatted, in-your-face Texan dude who'd introduced himself as Josiah Harrold, and his wife, Dilys, whose skin appeared to be stretched to the extreme, had been the icing on the whole cake.

"Does he know what you look like?" they'd asked Gabriel, almost as one person, which had been freaky.

Right in front of Cam. Right with Cam standing there

holding Gabriel's hand.

Gabriel hadn't hesitated, because Cam hadn't answered, so he'd made a show of leaning into Cam and smiling down at him.

"You don't need to see everything to know how you feel," he'd murmured, feeling Cam stiffen next to him.

Mr. Texas and his wife had wandered away after that.

"What was that?" Cam hissed under his breath.

"What?"

"How you feel? What the hell was that?"

"An answer to a question that you weren't going to reply to," Gabriel said.

"Well, stop it," Cam said. His voice was so low that Gabriel had to lean in to hear him. "Stop implying we feel things for each other. This is one fucking night."

Oh wow, Cam was really stressed, and it was Gabriel's job to help him out with that.

"Okay," he said. "My bad," he added, but he didn't let go of Cam's hand.

At least they were having dinner now, and the table they were at was family with extras. He was sitting next to a woman in her seventies with startlingly white hair and a propensity for patting his hand.

"How is Cameron?" she asked Gabriel with a little pat. Her voice was certainly loud enough for Cam to hear, and really she could be asking him directly. Her name was Poppy Stafford, and given that she wasn't on or near the top table, she was likely some kind of great-cousin or something. Who knew? He'd given up trying to follow everything a long time ago.

Gabriel nudged Cameron to indicate that Poppy was asking about him, but Cam was chatting to a teenager sitting on the other side of them and didn't even acknowledge the nudge. So that left Gabriel to answer the old lady's question.

"He's doing great," Gabriel said, then channeled his inner Cam and concentrated on his starter, a mix of lettuce with chicken. At least he thought it was chicken.

"Such a waste," Poppy continued, her voice even louder. "Don't you think?" she added, and Gabriel gave her a sideways glance.

"Sorry?" he asked, not sure he'd heard her right. He expected some comment about how all the good ones were gay; after all, she couldn't have failed to understand that Gabriel was there as Cam's partner tonight. She looked right at him with shrewd, focused eyes.

"Young Cameron," she began, and pointed right at him. "A waste. Such a shame."

That got Gabriel's back up. What did she mean by saying that in her loud voice? He'd observed a lot of that tonight. People nodding sadly as they spoke to Cam, tripping over their words like they didn't know what to say. Gabriel had even noticed a teenager talking *at* Cam, slowly and loudly, like being blind meant he couldn't hear or understand and the kid equated blindness with being dim. Cam had never flinched once. He clearly had the patience of a saint.

But then it got worse. The door to the ballroom opened and a couple walked in, heading for their table and taking the two seats that had been inexplicably empty.

"Evening, everyone," a dark-haired man announced dramatically to the table. "My apologies, the traffic was awful." He sat right opposite Gabriel, and his eyes landed right on where Gabriel and Cam were holding hands on the table.

"Hi, Cam." The slim, delicate-looking woman came toward Cam and kissed him first. "Sorry," she murmured, then took her seat next to the dark-haired man.

"Gabriel, this is my other sister, Sophie, and her husband, Mitchell."

Mitchell stood again and extended his hand across the table, and Gabriel momentarily released his hold of Cam's hand to lean over him to shake Mitchell's. Everything was so formal and stilted.

"I was just saying how much of a shame it is," Poppy said, sounding eager to expand on her comments with the new addition to the audience. "About his eyesight."

Cam stiffened next to him, and Gabriel took his hand again, this time under the table, squeezing it tight.

"Poppy—" Sophie began, then subsided when Mitchell frowned at her.

"When you and Mitchell have babies, they may be able to do a scan and you could make a decision about whether you want it," Poppy said, and Sophie went from flushed pink to scarlet. A hush fell over the table. "You know, if it's going to be blind."

What the fuck? Was this woman senile? That had to be the only explanation. If she was, then maybe a lot of people here tonight were impaired in the same way. Gabriel couldn't believe half of the shit Cam had endured. From the outright rude, who'd talked to him and not to Cam, to the over-interested, who'd touched him and used words like 'such a shame' and 'sorry'. Like Cam was something to be pitied.

Gabriel concluded several things at once. Nobody here tonight had any idea how to talk to Cam. Poppy was an aged bitch. Cam's sister Sophie was either pregnant or planning on it, because she was clutching her stomach. She also looked wary and startled when Mitchell leaned over to whisper in her ear.

He'd imagined that any sister of Cam's, half-sibling or not, would be different. Vivacious, maybe. But she was on edge and looked like she didn't want to be there. Gabriel watched them as they ate their meal. She didn't say much, and when she did speak, Mitchell was there, talking over her or belittling her. Of course, he was going for the good ol' boy effect, but all he was doing was making his wife sink lower in her chair.

And Gabriel knew exactly what was happening. It was exactly what Stefan did to him. But why did she put up with it? She probably had enough money to get a new husband and be a lot happier than she was now.

"And of course, having my beautiful wife there with me made everyone stare." Mitchell finished off a story about a business trip and pressed a kiss to Sophie's head, and she beamed up at him like he'd bestowed the best gift ever.

She would never want to leave him, not while he gave her rewards after making her feel like shit. Should he make a comment to Cam? Was it his place to point out that his sister was being treated that way? He'd bet Cam didn't even know; so much of any abuse was in touches and facial expressions. He closed his eyes briefly and listened to Mitchell wax lyrical about a *little* business that his *gorgeous* wife was starting. He sounded proud, but under it all there was a thread of possessiveness.

I only know that because I hear it all the time.

Next to him, Cam was trying not to be pissed, but

every line of him was taut with tension. It didn't help when Poppy carried on with her line of inappropriate comments.

"The balloons are beautiful shades of blue and gold, you know," she said, then leaned around Gabriel. "Do you remember blue?" she asked Cam.

Sophie looked wretched but said nothing. Mitchell snorted a laugh. He appeared to love drama, as he sat forward to wait for Cam's response.

Fuck it. Stefan would be mad at him, but Gabriel wasn't sitting there like an excuse for an idiot, and Cam shouldn't either.

"Cameron's vision loss is due to a one-in-a-million chance," he said, without any idea whether that was true. "He loves the color blue, which is the same as his gorgeous eyes. Sophie, it was nice to meet you, and congratulations on the pregnancy by the way. Poppy, we're very happy as a couple, thank you, and nothing stops us." She opened her mouth to say something, but Gabriel plunged ahead. "Also, planning for our Everest climb is well underway." Everest? Where was this shit coming from? "Isn't this event wonderful?"

Gabriel looked around the table at each person. Mitchell's mouth was hanging open, Sophie was cringing, and finally his gaze landed on Poppy, who looked a little shocked.

"Wonderful," she murmured.

For a few seconds the silence remained, then Poppy turned to Sophie and began to chat to her. Mitchell excused himself and headed for the top table, entering into some back slapping and hugs with Sebastian. A much different welcome to the son-in-law than the one Sebastian had shared with his biological son, Cam.

Strange, confusing family.

"Everest?" Cam said dryly, his voice only loud enough for Gabriel to hear.

"It was the first mountain I could think of," Gabriel admitted.

Education for him had stopped young, but he had Google, and hell, everyone knew Mount Everest.

"And my gorgeous blue eyes?"

"They are very blue and very gorgeous."

Cam spoke low to him again. "Is Sophie pregnant? She didn't tell me." He sounded disappointed. "But if you can tell, then she must be at least three months."

"No, flat as a pancake," Gabriel said. "But she has an incredibly expressive face, and she clutched her belly when Poppy made an ass of her old self. But that could have been a defensive move because her husband is all up in her face."

Cam shook his head. "What do you mean?"

"He's a judgmental prick," Gabriel muttered, then coughed. "Sorry."

"Like I said, family is off limits to you."

Gabriel couldn't let it alone, he didn't like the look of the way Cam's sister seemed so quiet and subservient. "What do you think of Mitchell?"

Gabriel had to ask, and he stared right at Cam, hoping to pick up some change in his expression.

"Sophie seems happy with him," he said. And that was all he was going to say about that, apparently.

"Where did he go? Mitchell, I mean." The way that Cam said "Mitchell", with a note of derision, added to Gabriel's initial suspicion that he and Cam weren't close.

Was anyone close in this crazy, mixed-up, who-is-related-to-whom family?

"Talking to your dad."

Cam huffed and picked up his water glass. "Now *that* I'd like to see," he murmured. "I bet it's all hugs and back-slaps and let's-take-over-the-universe-together over there."

"Pretty much." Gabriel sipped at his own water.

All that wine and champagne, and both of them were staying sober. He could manage that, but given the underlying mess of angst going on in the Stafford family, he thought it would be good for Cam to have a drink.

"So you don't get on with your dad?" Gabriel leaned in so he could talk low and hear the answer, and it crossed his mind that to anyone watching they would look like they were having a tender moment.

"We have differing opinions on my sight and my sexual orientation—"

"He's an asshole, then," Gabriel snapped, then nearly bit his lip. Somehow that visceral reaction had just slipped out, and the tightness in his chest at the rudeness of it was very real. He needed to be paid tonight, because otherwise how would he explain to Stefan what had happened? So he really needed to cool his jets.

But Cam didn't throw him out; he simply turned fully in his chair so he could face Gabriel. "What did you just say?"

"Sorry," Gabriel offered immediately.

"No, carry on, please." That could have sounded different, like Cam was patronizing him, but actually it was a genuine request. "What did you just say to me?"

Gabriel swallowed, and hesitated to find the right

answer.

"I just meant...we're at a family event, they're all unable to talk to you or look at you...hell, only a handful of people approach you normally, and your dad is the worst of all."

"And your point is?"

"Doesn't it piss you off?" Gabriel couldn't understand how Cam could sit there and keep his temper.

Cam looked straight at him, completely focused on the right point, and not for the first time Gabriel found himself fascinated by Cam's sapphire eyes.

"Can you pass me the wine?" Cam said finally.

Gabriel fought his initial instinct to pour wine for Cam, and instead passed him the nearest bottle of red. "Is red okay?"

Cam took the bottle, and Gabriel watched fascinated as Cam reached for his glass and filled it with wine. He balanced the bottle in his hand, and Gabriel noticed a subtle heft of it, probably testing for how much was in there and where the balancing point was. Cam used his other hand to hold the glass steady just off the table's surface. Everything about the way Cam worked was a matter of balance and center.

He took a healthy swallow of wine, and another, and another, then refilled the glass.

"Yes, of course it pisses me off," he murmured.

Cam looked nothing like his dad; he had a lot of his mom in him, and he didn't have the seemingly permanent expression of disapproval that marked Sebastian's face.

"Son, a word," Sebastian said from behind them.

Gabriel turned, and Mitchell was there as well, looking smug and arrogant. This wasn't good. He leaned close to Cam and whispered, "Mitchell is with him."

"I'm done here," Cam said, picked up the rest of the bottle of wine and the glass, and stood up. "Let's go," he said, and Gabriel scrambled to stand, taking the nearly full glass from him and offering his arm.

As quickly as he could, he led Cam through the maze of tables and to the door they'd come in through, and from there to the elevators. Only when they were inside with the doors closing on an irate-looking Sebastian heading toward them could Gabriel finally relax a little.

Cam stood against the opposite side of the car, the bottle of wine hugged to his chest and his expression strangely impassive.

The elevator came to a stop on the top floor and Cam strode out, Gabriel behind him, trailing him to his apartment.

Then they went inside, and finally they were alone.

CHAPTER 8

Cam had never once given his father the satisfaction of backing down or walking away. That was what the bastard wanted. For the son he perceived as weak in so many ways to step aside. Didn't matter that the Dallas Stafford Royal was the best performing of the Stafford hotels, didn't matter that the life Cam had been born into had been his training ground.

Nope. All Sebastian Stafford saw was that Cam was damaged goods. Gay, blind, useless.

And he never, ever let it get to him.

Only, he'd always dealt with it on his own. He'd never taken a date or a friend to a family event, not even ex-from-hell Adam, the bastard who'd fucked him over. So it didn't matter what people said to him. Didn't affect him to be told that people were sorry for him, or that tragedy was a terribly tragic thing in an awfully, tragically blind kind of way. Pity was shitty to keep having to take at these things, but it was okay. No one else heard their shit. No one else judged him.

But tonight this stranger in his life had heard it all, and judged him, and Cam was ashamed.

He'd let these things slide for so long that he'd never even thought about how it all looked.

He reached out a hand for the glass with the wine in it, and Gabriel, this man he'd hired, knew to pass it to him and wait for Cam to grasp it properly. He downed that glass in one, and it joined the first glass in burning a nice warm trail to his belly. He knew the bottle in his hand only had one more glass in it, so he poured that and placed it on the coffee table before sitting on the sofa.

"You can go; you're done," he announced. "The rest of your money is in the paper wallet on the table by the front door. Six counted and verified it, so we'll know if you're trying to fuck us over." Gidget jumped up on the sofa next to him and nosed at his neck; he gave her a reassuring pat. He sounded like an ass and he knew it.

Then he waited for the familiar sounds of someone leaving his apartment, but Gabriel appeared to be opening his fridge and taking out a bottle of whatever in there was fizzy, because he heard the hiss of escaped gas as it was opened.

"You can go," he repeated. "You're done."

"We have another hour," Gabriel answered, and sat down on the sofa opposite Cam.

"Call it a bonus to get home early," Cam suggested.

"I like it here. I'm staying here."

Fuck. This was yet more pity, and no wonder after everything Gabriel had heard tonight.

"I have Six on speed dial," Cam warned him.

"Jeez, I want to sit on your comfy sofa, drinking Sprite and chatting, and you want to sic your guard dog on me? Dude, that is harsh."

A small knot of something collected in his chest. Not panic or fear, but maybe nerves. Was Gabriel acting in a threatening way? Six had warned him that if the hooker wouldn't leave, he would deal with it. He'd also insisted on locking away anything valuable.

Six looked out for him all the time, but at this particular moment, Cam desperately wanted to feel like he was in control, like he could handle it.

Gabriel was something he hadn't been expecting. He talked softly, was just there by his side, smelling delicious and turning Cam on. A couple of times this evening the nebulous concept of paying for sex as well had been hovering just out of reach of his rational thoughts.

He needed sex just like the next man, and every time Gabriel pressed into him, the reassuring weight and solid form of him in reach, Cam was aroused. The scent of Gabriel was intoxicating, and the sound of his voice was enough to make Cam want to touch.

The last man he'd touched in any way other than shaking hands had been Adam, and look how that had ended.

"What do you want to talk about?" he asked finally.

"You have a complicated family."

"Family is always complicated," he muttered, then realized what he'd said. If the story that Gabriel had used tonight was true, then that had been an insensitive thing to say, even to someone who sold himself for a living.

"How much of what you said tonight about your family life and history was true?"

Gabriel chuckled and moved on the sofa, the knock of his half-full plastic bottle on the table. "I never knew my dad, so him passing away young was a stretch. For all I know he could still be walking around on the wrong side of the tracks in Laredo peddling whatever it was that drew my mom to him. Drugs, sex, who knows."

"Your mom was a…"

"No, not like me, no way. She was a dreamer, all rainbows and hippie shit, always saw the best in people, ended up with me and a crap job on a ranch outside Laredo. We had it good for a few years, and then she died.

Pretty quickly, actually—cancer, we think, although we didn't have the money for testing or fixing, you know what I mean? She was beautiful. I always thought she was beautiful; she died still so beautiful."

Compassion swelled inside Cam. Cancer was a horrible way to lose a parent. His mom might be in a constant state of battle with his dad and his dad's new wife over everything but, at least she was in his life and actually cared about him, which was more than his dad did.

"I'm sorry," he offered, without a hint of the pity he hated hearing all the time. "How old were you?"

Gabriel didn't answer straight away. "Ten," he finally said, his tone a curious mix of sadness and anger.

"And you stayed on the ranch? Or did you end up…" Leaving and living on the streets. Cam would be the first to admit he knew very little about the motivations of a man who chose to sell his body for money.

"I stayed," Gabriel said. "Can I ask you a question?"

Ah, so that was a touchy subject, and one that Cam was happy to leave alone. A man was entitled to privacy, after all. Which was why the concept of a question from Gabriel had him wincing inside.

"I can't promise to answer."

"People have probably asked this before, but can you see in your dreams?"

Wow, that was a deep question. "I didn't start to go blind until I was twelve, and I have images in my head, so yeah, I still have pictures in my dreams."

"Do you ever feel you miss out in life, or do you take it all in your stride?"

"Jeez, what is this? Twenty question? I feel like I

experience *differently*, no less or more, so no, I don't think I miss out. I might not be able to see, but that doesn't mean I'm emotionally blind."

"Wow, that's deep."

"You asked."

"Well, how do you know where your mouth is when you're eating? I mean, I watched you pour wine, for god's sake, into a glass, and you were balancing the wine, testing its weight—is that how it works?"

"My mouth is where everyone else's is, and it's instinct, and yeah, to pour a drink it's useful to find a center of balance and have the glass in your other hand, and then it's a matter of pouring carefully."

The sofa moved on the other side of him to Gidget, and Cam realized that Gabriel had moved to sit closer to him. Why would he do that?

Gabriel sighed. "I guess you find some people condescending?"

"Frequently."

"Like they expect you not to be able to do things?"

"Uh-huh." Cam was running out of things to say here.

"How can you have sexual thoughts about a man if you can't see him and don't know what he looks like?"

These questions were changing slowly each time, becoming way more personal than Cam wanted to answer. He could feel himself closing down emotionally, like he always did when he was worried about adding another vulnerability for others to see.

"I don't judge people by how they look," he offered, simple and to the point.

"So you don't have the prejudices others have, then."

"That's not entirely true. I have a whole other set of

criteria—voice, sense of humor, intelligence, politeness, the smell of a man, the way he touches me or I touch him. I'm the first person to judge, and actually use more criteria than just assuming that what a person wears or what they look like is what defines them." He stopped for a moment and appeared to be considering what to say. "Meekness, hesitance, arrogance…they all come through in tone and choice of words. Maybe you'll see a gorgeous man and think he's hot because of a fortunate mix of genetics—eye color, build, hair—but really maybe he looks hot because he's hot from the inside out."

Gabriel moved on the sofa, knocking Cam's leg and touching a hand to that point in apology. Cam could have him tonight—he could ask for what he'd essentially paid for. It had been months since he'd last had a man's mouth on him. His cock got into the image and began to harden, and he hoped to hell it would stop, because the last thing he needed was to get turned on right here and now. In fact Gabriel really needed to leave. He took another healthy swallow of red wine, and the faint buzz in his head and the softness in his limbs told him he'd reached that perfect point where he was all warm and mellow but still had control over his inhibitions.

After tonight he needed that.

"I bet even you would fall for someone where the beauty was only skin deep." Gabriel rested a hand on Cam's thigh, his thumb tracing patterns on the material of Cam's pants.

"Stop doing that," Cam said, and made a shooing motion with his free hand. He could have pushed the hand away, but he liked it, so his physical side was winning over his sane, rational thoughts. Didn't matter, because

Gabriel ignored him, the thumb pushing a little harder, the hand moving just that tiny bit higher.

"My ex had that issue. He was a good actor."

"I think we're all one big mess of insecurity about the world and what image and attractiveness mean. People who pay me can look beyond the fact that they're paying for sex, and instead they talk about my eyes, or my lips, or my ass."

The reminder of who and what he was should have been enough for Cam to switch off this dangerous, tantalizing need that coiled inside him. It wasn't, and Gabriel was still talking, his voice mesmerizing.

"I have this one client, you know, he likes me to push him into the shower, tie his hands behind his back and make him kneel, then order him to tell me what he thinks of me. He says I'm beautiful, that my eyes are the color of coal, that my face is all angles and my lips are pouty. He talks about my nipples and how they need to be sucked and how my belly is flat and it's that perfection that gets him hard. I look in the mirror and I don't see what he says about me, though."

Fuck. Cam was getting harder now, and it had to be obvious. "What do you do then?" The image of being on his knees, his hands tied behind his back, was a thing of beauty. He could imagine kneeling, looking up at the man who was tracing those patterns on his legs, higher and higher.

Looking. No. But at least feeling the bite of rope on his wrists, completely in the dark, the power that would give the other man; hell, the power it would give him. He could bite on his lip, tell Gabriel exactly what he thought of him.

"What do I do when?" Gabriel was close now, his lips right by Cam's ear, the breath soft on his skin as Gabriel spoke.

"After he's told you that, what happens next?"

"I turn the water on. He wants to feel that on his skin, which is so soft, impossibly soft." Gabriel's hand finally rested over Cam's cock, and he squeezed the rigid length firmly before slipping a hand up to open his fly. "I order him to suck me, right under the water, and he struggles to breathe. It's like heaven looking down at him, struggling, his eyes closed, his mouth wrapped around my cock."

He slipped a hand under material, inside Cam's shorts, and circled his cock.

"And?" Cam asked, a little breathless.

"He tries to rub off against my leg, but I push him away. He has to come on his own—no hands, just what's in his head."

"What are you doing?" Cam asked, a little breathless as Gabriel cleverly twisted his hands around the length of him.

"If you have to ask," Gabriel said, "I'm doing it wrong." He closed his teeth around Cam's lobe, tugged at it, and Cam was torn between hearing Gabriel's voice and needing that small tug of pain to finish him off.

"Tell me how he comes," he said, his mind one mess of need.

Gabriel chuckled, gave one last tug at the lobe. "I reach down and I twist my fingers in his hair. He wants me to fuck his mouth—he's asked me for it before, and I hate being held like that, but he wants me to stop him moving, and then he's coming so fucking hard. I feel every pulse as his body bucks, and he's gasping around my cock, and I don't let him breathe."

And that was it, game over, Cam was pushed right over the edge into orgasm just by words and fingers alone. Right there in his best suit pants, right over the hand of the hooker he'd hired for the night. He waited for shame, but there was none.

He'd paid for that, and Gabriel had been doing his job.

"What about you?" Cam murmured, his breathing ragged.

"What about me?"

"In the shower, with this guy, do you come in his mouth, on his face?"

The answer was slow in coming, and not before Gabriel had released his hold on Cam's cock and padded to the bathroom to wash his hands, coming back with a cloth and wiping at Cam as best he could. "I don't get off unless someone pays me for to get off; that's extra."

Something about the way Gabriel phrased that was wrong, just off, and it didn't sit right.

"You don't come unless someone pays you to come."

"That's right. Time's up," Gabriel murmured, and rose from the sofa, leaning over and fussing over Gidget. On the way up, he pressed a gentle kiss to Cam's lips. "Watch out for your sister Sophie. I don't like the way she is with Mitchell. And don't let your family drag you down," he said.

And then he left.

* * * * *

Gabriel had done something to him.

Not just given him a handjob with added dirty story, which still didn't fail to get him off whenever he replayed it.

Not just created a fantasy in which Gabriel and he were climbing Mount Everest.

But made sex a frame of reference for Cam in which he'd tasted something with Gabriel that could well become an addiction.

He had money. Gabriel gave handjobs for money. In Cam's head, that was a match made in heaven.

And really that was all he could think about as he sat in the conference room a full two days after the engagement party. Close family were still in the hotel, and unfortunately that meant his dad was still there, although he was going back up to Chicago that evening.

Cam had tried to avoid the inevitable, but as fast as he was, he couldn't outrun his dad.

"So we'd like to talk to you about the Royal."

Cam stayed quiet. He was there with his dad and his idiot brother-in-law Mitchell. What Sophie saw in Mitchell, he didn't know. The man was seriously shifty, and he wasn't entirely sure that his sister was actually happy, which Gabriel had also alluded to. Who was he to judge, though? Not like he was in a serious relationship.

Or like he was getting sex, even.

"We'd like to work with you," Mitchell said, so earnestly that it set Cam's teeth on edge. "Take some of the load off you; make your life easier."

"There will come a time when you won't be able to run this hotel," Cam's dad interjected.

"It's a long time until I'm seventy, Dad," Cam said. He leaned back in his chair and crossed his arms over his chest. Okay, so it was a defensive position, but it was also an effective way to hold in his temper.

"Don't be smart," Sebastian Stafford snapped. That

was what he did when he was being less *dad* and more *hotel owner*. Only this wasn't Sebastian's place to do with as he wanted, and certainly nothing to do with Mitchell.

"No help needed, thank you," Cam said, and pushed himself up from the table. "Are we done now?"

"Sebastian?" Mitchell asked, confused. No doubt Sebastian had sold his favorite son-in-law, the normal son he'd never had, the idea that him running this hotel was a shoo-in.

"Sit down, Cameron," his dad snapped.

"Too busy, Sebastian." He deliberately didn't use the word "Dad", didn't want to personalize this more than he had to.

"Sit the hell down."

"I have a meeting—"

"Mitchell, leave us, please," Sebastian ordered. "And you, Cameron, wait there."

The door shut, and for a second Cam cursed his lack of sight. He had to assume that Mitchell had left and wasn't standing in a corner watching. He concentrated hard on the noises and scents in the room, relieved to smell that Mitchell's expensive and cloying cologne was diminishing.

"You have five minutes," Cam said.

"Ever since Adam left, we've been worried about the future of the Royal, son. For his faults, he worked well at being your support network."

"Adam who stole from the hotel, and me, and lied to everyone he met? That Adam?"

His dad ignored that. "Still, you're alone here, and vulnerable to any and all perverted men who want to steal from you—"

"What the hell?"

"That man at the party, who was he?"

"A friend."

"He was staring at everyone. How well do you know him?"

"I know him very well, and you wouldn't believe the observations he made to me about what was going on at that party."

"You mean he was your spy?"

"No, Dad, I didn't mean that at all."

"Whatever," Sebastian continued. "I just feel it would make sense to bring in a co-manager."

"You mean Mitchell."

"Yes."

"No," Cam said, and that was the end of it. But Sebastian had other ideas.

"I wouldn't want to involve the legal team in insisting that you have help."

And there it was. The threat that Cam had been expecting. He wasn't going to rise to it. The hotel had been left to him by his grandfather, bypassing the great Sebastian Stafford, who had recommended that Cam be cut out of the usual inheritance of a hotel and given cash instead.

No sense in him losing out, give him the money, but a blind man running a hotel, for god's sake, how will that work?

Oh yeah, he remembered that conversation very well, sitting in the office of the lawyers who'd handled Grandpa Stafford's estate. Sebastian had talked about him like him being blind meant he couldn't hear every single word.

He headed for the door, ignored the curse from his

dad, and muscled his way past a surprised Mitchell.

"We only want the best for you," Mitchell called after him.

Jesus, it was hard not to turn around and flatten the moron.

He headed straight for the security office and the reassurance of Six, whom he knew was on his side. Six wasn't there, but if Cam sat there long enough, he'd be back.

"What's happened?" Six said from the doorway. "Who do I have to kill?"

Cam smiled at that. "A stubborn idiot and an entitled ass."

"So basically your dad and your brother-in-law. I can do that. Might be difficult to hide two bodies at the same time, but there's construction all over the city. It can be done."

Cam heard a chair move, imagined Six as he'd known him fifteen years before. Tall, strong, he'd been brought in by the family as a personal bodyguard after an attempt at kidnapping one of the Stafford kids had been foiled. Then, when Cam's eyesight had deteriorated, Six had become Cam's protector, and then friend. He used to turn chairs and straddle them with his arms on the back, and that was how Cam was picturing him now.

"How much gray do you have in your hair now?" Cam asked.

"Enough so I look devastatingly sexy," Six snarked back at him.

They laughed together, the stress of Cam's dad slowly slipping back to where it belonged.

"I need to get on to Charlie and make sure the terms of

grandpa's will are still airtight."

Charlie had been the family lawyer, but Cam had outbid his dad a long time ago to retain Charlie's services.

"Shit, Cam, not that again."

"Yeah. Implication is at some point I'll want to give up the Royal, that I won't be able to cope." He air-quoted the word "cope" and sighed noisily. "He wants Mitchell to co-manage, despite the Royal being the most financially lucrative boutique hotel that the Stafford's run."

He rolled his neck and heard the crack, feeling the tension slip a little. This was why he hated family events at his hotel, but given that Chloe had chosen to go to college in Dallas, then fallen in love with Luke at an event at this hotel, it was inevitable that the Dallas Stafford Royal would be the center of celebrations.

"Okay, so we check with Charlie. Nothing has changed since last time we all met up." Six spoke confidently, but Cam hadn't been totally honest with his best friend. The small amount of peripheral vision he had was becoming more blurry.

Inevitable degeneration, they said to him. Was that enough for someone to insist he had to leave the Royal?

I couldn't handle that.

"Can I ask you another question? It's about Sophie."

"Your sister Sophie? What about her?"

"Gabriel said something about Mitchell, about how we should look out for Sophie." Six stayed suspiciously quiet, and dread began to build. "What aren't you telling me, Six?"

"I don't like Mitchell with her, I think since they married she's got quieter, and sometimes..." He trailed away, and Cam grew impatient.

"What? For god's sake, Six."

"I think he has a hold on her that I don't like."

Cam thought for a moment. "Find out more. I want to know what's going on."

"That could be a can of worms you could never put the lid back on."

"I don't care, she's my sister."

"On it."

"Also, I need the number for Gabriel."

"Why?"

"Because I do." How was that for a snappy comeback?

Six huffed. "What are you, four? Give me your phone."

Cam passed over his phone and there were some noises—beeps from the phone, soft curses about Gabriel's parentage from Six, and Cam's own breathing, which was loud in his ears.

"There, but I'm fucked off with you for wanting it." That was Six, cutting to the chase with a complete lack of respect. Which meant Cam had to be completely honest right back at him.

"Six, I'm fucked off with myself."

"Then why do it?"

"Because there's something there—heat and desire and need and something forbidden."

Six huffed again. He was doing a lot of that at the moment. "I will label this your hooker stage, and we will never refer to it again after you're done."

He meant it for real. Six was very good at compartmentalizing his emotions.

Back in his room, Gidget next to him, his hands buried

in her fur, Cam decided that until his dad and Mitchell had gone, he would be taking Gidget with him everywhere. Just so she could bite either of them if needed.

He scrolled to his sister's number listening for the code for her entry; he just wanted to let her know he was there for her. She didn't answer.

"This is all shitty," he said as he scruffed Gidget's neck. She nosed at his leg and said nothing back to him. Which was a good call, because he had so much inside him that needed to come out.

"The one thing I can't handle is pity," he murmured to her, and she butted his leg again. "I've had enough pity to last me a lifetime. You know what I need right now? To fuck someone, to be fucked, to replace the shit in my head with sex. Is that wrong?"

This time Gidget laid her head on his leg, and he knew she would drool on his pants.

That was the least of his worries.

CHAPTER 9

"Hey, baby, you awake?"

Gabriel turned over in bed, his left knee twisting in the covers, the twinge of pain enough to remind him that he needed to stretch out before doing anything dramatic like getting out of bed.

"Yeah," he called, and shuffled to sit upright a bit more. He wanted to be respectful to Stefan and give him the attention he deserved. It wouldn't be right to be slouching about in bed when Stefan was probably bringing in coffee and toast, or something like that anyway.

Stefan pushed in with a mug in one hand, mail under his arm, and his iPad in the other.

"I have something to show you," Stefan said, and sat on the side of the bed. "The money came in from that client at the Stafford Hotel."

"Good."

"He sent us a lot of money, more than I was expecting. You know anything about why he'd do that?"

"No," Gabriel said.

"What did you quote him when you agreed to it all? It's a lot of money sitting in the account." Stefan sounded proud, and Gabriel smiled at him. There was nothing better than breakfast in bed with Stefan talking over how well Gabriel had done in the few days previous.

"Six hundred; I never thought he'd take it," Gabriel said.

"Six hundred, eh? For four hours."

"Yeah."

"He's sent us a thousand—that's some tip."

Stefan reached out a hand and circled Gabriel's wrist, and Gabriel knew better than to pull away even when it tightened fractionally and burned a little. Stefan rubbed his thumb over the scar there, right on the wrist.

"I did a good job," Gabriel defended himself. And he had. He'd played his part, and Cam had seemed happy when Gabriel left. Added to which he'd come all over Gabriel's hand and the expression of bliss on his face when he'd peaked was something Gabriel could keep locked away in his head. The expression had been pure pleasure, untouched by darkness in any way.

"You were his escort, his companion. No sex, right?"

"Stefan—"

"The parameters agreed, the rules we listed before this, said that there would be no sex, like he asked."

"I know, but—"

"What did you do, Gabriel?" The grip on his wrist tightened and fear flared inside him. He'd done this, fucked up again, gone against what Stefan had said. Why did he even think he could make decisions like that for himself?

"He was pissed off with his family, so I gave him a handjob and got him off."

The hand holding his wrist flew up and slapped him around the face, the coffee in his hand slopping over the side and onto his bare chest. He couldn't help it, he yelped, a strange, twisted sound that he couldn't keep in. Stefan hated it when he made a noise. Another slap pushed his head back to the headboard, and he tried to put the coffee away from him only to have it yanked from his hand. Another slap turned into more of a punch, right on his shoulder, and he moved sideways in the bed, his trapped knee twisting.

"Fucking idiot," Stefan snapped. "You break the fucking rules and no one will want your ass, not even me."

"Stef—"

"If he doesn't repeat request, then it's your fault for fucking off a cash cow, you stupid fucking idiot."

Another hit. This one connected with his chest. And there was more shouting. "You want to go live on that fucking farm with all the other victims? Huh? You want to go stay with Kyle who writes to you about horses and barns? You want to give up the chance of a new life and shovel shit for the rest of your life?"

Stefan yanked back the covers, exposing his naked body to the cold air.

"No, I don't," Gabriel said. He writhed away from Stefan, but Stefan was bigger, stronger, and filled with righteous anger, and Gabriel knew this was all his fault. He shouldn't have fallen for sapphire eyes and a sad expression; he should have done what Stefan had agreed to and left.

Stefan shoved his iPad to the floor and straddled Gabriel, pinning his hands above his head and holding them there with one of his hands. With his free hand, he circled Gabriel's throat.

"I don't want to," Gabriel said.

"Did I not make it clear?" Stefan snarled. "Was I not one hundred percent fucking clear about what you needed to do? You were a broken soul, and I saved you, and you repay me with this shit?"

He pressed hard against Gabriel's windpipe, held his hand there, his eyes inches from Gabriel's and his mouth constantly moving. Gabriel's vision blurred and darkened. Was this what it was like for Cam? Pure, blue-eyed Cam, with his broken gaze. Gabriel could see spots, knew he was losing consciousness, and only at that moment did he stop struggling.

He hadn't been wrong. What he'd done for Cam had been because he'd known he could make someone else's pain vanish. *It's not wrong. I wasn't wrong.*

Silence, and Stefan was climbing off him, wiping at the mess he'd left coming on Gabriel's belly.

"Look what you made me do," he said with genuine regret in his tone. Then he pressed a kiss to Gabriel's forehead. "I'll make you a new coffee, baby," he added.

And he left.

Gabriel wanted to curl onto his side and cry, but if Stefan was coming back…he needed to move.

Then he saw the letter on the floor, addressed to him, the envelope torn open. Another letter from Legacy Ranch. He reached over to push it under the bed. There couldn't be an excuse to upset Stefan anymore.

That move had the cum on his belly pooling and sliding off onto the covers. He wiped at the mess with the corner of the sheet, knowing he would put every piece of fabric on this bed in the wash. Stefan never usually got angry like that inside Gabriel's bedroom; not in his sanctuary.

Stefan came in, all smiles, flinging open the curtains to a bright new day, talking about their healthy bank balance and how Gabriel's percentage would be nearly two hundred dollars.

That wasn't much, but he had fucked up.

Now if only Cam would call again; then he could

make everything right with Stefan.

"Remember you've nothing booked for today. You may want to get yourself ready and get out into the real world. You can't stay in bed forever." He tutted and crossed his arms over his chest. "Can't have you going out looking like you got into a fight. I'm out for the rest of the day. Have fun."

Stefan left, and only thirty minutes after the front door slammed did he dare to pull out the letter; it was dated two days ago and in different handwriting than usual, although the tone of it suggested the same author, maybe dictating. He read on.

Gabriel, this is Jason, Kyle hurt his hand yesterday and had to have stitches which makes it all kinds of painful for him to hold a pen. The idiot. I told him not to try and pull that nail out of the wood without protection, but no, he had to do it anyway. Anyway, he's sitting next to me so I have to write what he says. Some guy turned up looking for Mistry yesterday. Said he'd lost her and did we have her, and Kyle called up to the house and Darren and Jack came down and went all bad ass on him. I didn't like the guy, looked a bit shifty, but Kyle said we should try and be polite. Sometimes I think Kyle is too nice for his own good.

Ouch, Kyle just smacked me one. The ass. So, yeah, picture this, Jack is saying that it was convenient that this guy wanted Mistry back after we'd all spent time and thousands of dollars on getting her all fixed up. Darren added that he could give a full accounting of the costs that would need to be repaid, and Jack said that as soon as the guy handed over papers of proof, and a check, that he could have Mistry back. He left, but I think he's trouble, watch this space.

Kyle just told me to write to tell you to visit, like he does all the time.

He just smacked me again, I swear, this is getting out of hand. But you gotta love the guy.

Anyway, that's the latest news, and Kyle says hi, and more next week.

The letter was signed with a scrawl that looked something like the name Jason. This was letter thirty-three. They'd begun to arrive a year ago, charting Kyle and Jason's messy, happy home life on a ranch.

Gabriel ached with the need to see the place, but he would never go.

Seeing the name Darren there was too much. It had been Darren's brother Hank who had abused Gabriel at the Bar Five Ranch, and Darren had sent a check to Gabriel to pay him off. The letter with it had spoken of sorrow and guilt, and how Darren would always be there if Gabriel needed him.

Fuck that.

Stefan had taken the letter and the check, cashed the check, and laughed when he burned the letter.

"Like anyone else cares about you the same as me," he'd said.

So no, Gabriel didn't want to hear what Darren *fucking* Castille was doing.

He showered and dressed, making sure his clothes covered whatever bruises there were. They'd be gone soon; not much marked his sun-bronzed skin. And all the time he thought about the ranch, and Stefan, and that pure, perfect moment when every care and worry had disappeared from Cam's face as he was coming.

He wasn't ever going to Legacy Ranch.

I'm not going there. Stefan needs me. Stefan saved me.

Then he caught sight of a bruise he couldn't cover, high on his forehead—nothing too obvious, but he could see it if he looked closely enough.

Stefan pulled me from that street corner and brought me home. Gave me food. Gave me a bed. Saved me.

He picked up a jacket and left the apartment, his cell in his pocket and no destination in mind. Sometimes he liked to walk the streets of Dallas, dressed in his smart jeans and nice shirt, but today he wanted to get into a different headspace. He stopped for a coffee, sitting with a whole load of tourists all taking selfies in front of the building which, he picked up, had been used in an episode of *Dallas* way back in the eighties. For the longest time he nursed his coffee and people-watched and tried really hard not to think of anything.

But that wasn't possible, because he had too much to think about that he couldn't push to one side.

When he thought back to the day of the trial, he just remembered crying.

The words had been there, explaining what had happened to him, and he recalled seeing the two others who had suffered at the hands of a sadistic bastard—a young kid, Daniel, and a man older than him, Kyle. Neither of them had cried.

But Gabriel had cried when he arrived there, cried as he spoke, and sobbed in the car afterward.

Stefan had held his hand in the car, driving one-handed and reassuring him that everything was going to be okay. He'd even bought Gabriel a suit.

"You have to look like a normal person, Angel," he'd said as he'd knotted Gabriel's tie before they left the apartment. The tie had hurt because the bruising on his neck was new, and Gabriel always knew that was when the crying started.

Stefan said he looked so pretty when he cried, talked about his dark eyes being soft.

"Is anyone sitting here?" A voice broke into his reverie, and he looked up into the face of a kid, no more than ten or so, with a family behind him.

"I was just leaving," Gabriel lied, and stood up, picking up his cup and then wondering what the hell to do with the delicate china he'd been given. He went back inside and placed the cup on the counter, then left, walking past the family of four—mom, dad, two sons—laughing over something on a phone in the middle of the table.

Familiar feelings of envy rose to the surface, and he pushed them away. He hadn't ever needed a dad, or a brother, but he'd loved his mom.

Now he loved Stefan, and if he wasn't careful Stefan wouldn't be part of his world. Getting those letters from Kyle was causing a problem. At first Stefan had been intrigued, telling Gabriel he should make an effort with the obscenely rich Campbell-Hayes family, adding that they owed Gabriel. How he figured that, Gabriel didn't know, and he'd said so. He had a tenuous connection to Darren, who worked for them, and that was it.

Ever since then, when a letter arrived there was a rage in Stefan that scared Gabriel.

The letters needed to stop.

He pulled out his cell and the last letter, which was

folded in his pocket, and with no thought other than to make it all stop, he dialed the number written carefully at the top of the paper. The phone rang three times, and relief began to manifest in his chest when it seemed that there was no one to answer. Then the ringing stopped and the call connected.

"Legacy Ranch," a voice announced.

"I need to talk to Kyle," Gabriel said before he could second-guess himself.

"Kyle! Phone for you!"

There was a clatter as the phone was clearly dumped somewhere—a table, or a counter, or the floor, maybe. Then another noise as it was picked up.

"Kyle Braden. Can I help?"

Kyle had a soft voice. Gabriel remembered the tone from the trial. The skinny guy had had green eyes that were sunken, and he'd looked gaunt and exhausted. The only part of the story of his life that Gabriel knew was the fact that they'd both suffered at the hands of Hank Castille.

"You have to stop writing those letters," Gabriel snapped.

There was a moment of silence, then Kyle spoke. "Gabriel, is that you?"

"Stop writing the letters. My friend Stefan doesn't like it."

"It's real nice to hear from you," Kyle said. His tone was less business and warmer now, the cadence of it soothing.

"Stop. Okay?"

More silence, and the noise that had been in the background vanished; seemed Kyle had shut himself in somewhere quiet.

"How are you doing?" Kyle asked.

Why the hell did Kyle want to know that?

"Stop writing them, understand?"

Before he could second-guess himself, he ended the call, then stared at his cell with abrupt disbelief of what he'd just done. Stefan would be pissed if he found out; he'd explicitly said that if Gabriel ever contacted anyone at Legacy, he needed to manage what Gabriel said. Stefan knew best, so why had Gabriel even thought it would be a good idea to call?

Because this is my life. Because I have bruises.

An incoming text scared the shit out of him so much that he almost dropped the phone because he'd been so deep in thought.

The message was simple.

Are you free? I want to book you this afternoon. Who was this from? And then another text from the same number. *Cameron Stafford. Sorry, forgot to say that.*

Gabriel's first instinct was to say no. He didn't want to open himself up to seeing Cam in any way, but he knew Stefan would want to comment on this.

He fired off a quick text to Stefan to ask if Cam was a client he wanted Gabriel to see. Stefan answered immediately.

Do it and don't fuck it up. Leave him wanting more.

Gabriel looked at the time, added on an hour to get himself ready, then texted a time to Cam.

Half of him expected the return text to be a negotiation on something—time, more about money, questions about Gabriel—but all the that came back from Cam was a reminder of the room number.

People walked past his hiding place on their way to wherever they were going. Work, or maybe they were heading up to Klyde Warren Park, but they all had purpose. And he bet none of them had a purpose that included being paid for sex in the afternoon.

He straightened his back, rolled his neck, and pocketed his cell.

Show time.

He knocked on the door and heard Cam on the other side call, "Come in." He tried the handle, thinking that was some kind of wind-up, but the door opened. He didn't know what he was expecting to see inside. Some of his clients were already buck naked, some dressed in an approximation of what they considered sexy, but Cam? He was on the floor with Gidget on his stomach and they were fighting over a chew toy. He shouldn't find it cute, but he did. Gidget was a nice dog, reminded him of the dogs on the ranch when he'd been a kid.

When his mom had still been alive.

Before it had all gone to hell.

Cam rolled up into a standing position and Gidget stood at his side, both of them looking right at Gabriel.

"Hey," Cam said, and brushed at his chest. His black T-shirt, all kinds of casual, emblazoned with a logo that included a faded rainbow and writing, was covered in dog hair. "How's that?" he asked, spreading his arms, and Gabriel wasn't sure what he needed to comment on. Was it the shirt, the dog hair, the muscles of Cam's arms, or the fact that Cam was fucking gorgeous?

"How's what?" That seemed like a safe question.

"Did I get all the hair off?"

Gabriel moved closer. "Nope," he said, and wondered if he should be brushing it away.

Cam laughed at that, and in a smooth move he pulled the T-shirt off and gripped it in one hand. "I need a clean shirt," he announced.

But Gabriel wasn't listening, not really. Cam wasn't built or muscle bound, he was slim, his chest hair the same blond as his hair, his cinnamon nipples slightly erect, probably due to the AC that blasted into the room, counteracting the heat outside. And the hair below his navel disappeared into the band of his loose sweats. Those same sweats hung on his hips, his stomach flat, and in there, hidden away, was something that Gabriel couldn't forget.

The weight and feel of Cam's sex was the stuff of his fantasies at the moment. That and the look on the man's face.

"Is everything okay?" Cam asked a little uncertainly.

"Yeah?"

"Sorry, you're just super quiet. Hang there a minute." He walked confidently past the sofa and through a door, coming back a little later pulling a new T-shirt over his head, this a Dallas Cowboys one.

"How do you know what you're wearing?" Gabriel blurted out before he could stop himself. He should keep his mouth shut. Stefan was right; when Gabriel asked stupid questions, he didn't just embarrass himself, but Stefan as well.

But Cam didn't seem fazed by the question.

"I have this system. First off Six describes everything, and then everything in my closet is grouped by type, so you know, button-downs in one place, T-shirts in another, and then there's this." He came closer to Gabriel and stopped. "Feel this."

He held out a hand, and Gabriel took it, allowing himself to be guided to touch a raised profile of bumps in the hem of the T.

"Is that braille?"

"Yep. Tells me this is a Cowboys shirt, and it's dark blue. Right?"

"Yeah." All Gabriel could think was that Cam was real close, and that the scent of him was so familiar that Gabriel was actually feeling the low pull of arousal. That hadn't happened in forever.

Cam stepped back, and Gabriel wanted to follow, but he didn't.

"Money," Cam announced, and crossed to a bureau, pulling out an envelope. "Should cover me into the evening." Then he frowned. "Unless you're already booked out tonight."

Gabriel took the envelope and opened it. *Always count the money.* There was enough there for a midnight finish—a lot of money.

"No, you have me for the rest of the day."

"Okay then," Cam said with a grin. "Come on."

Gabriel was flustered after all these years; faced with that smile, he'd forgotten his job. He needed to negotiate what was happening here, but he'd lost the power of speech. Gidget had given up and padded into the kitchen, and just that small barrier between them was gone now.

"What do you want?" Gabriel asked, professional and to the point.

Cam tilted his head. "As much as we can fit in," he said. "I need to get you out of my head, and I really need to get off."

Okay, a transaction like that was one Gabriel could handle. He stepped up into Cam's space and fisted his T-shirt. His part of this deal was to start things off using what he'd learned about Cam, and the biggest thing was the talking.

"You want me to make you feel good?" he asked.

His voice sounded a little alien to him, like he wasn't putting all his effort into it, and that single thought made him angry with himself. Frustrated that he couldn't get into character, he yanked at Cam, then began to push him back, right up against the wall by the bedroom door. Cam let out a soft *oomph* as he hit the wall but he didn't yank himself away. Gabriel moved up close, pressing his weight against Cam.

"You shouldn't have bothered putting your shirt on," he said, and lifted it up over Cam's head and tossed it to the floor.

Actually faced with being able to touch Cam properly, he forgot what he needed to do next.

Nipples, belly, lower, cock, done.

But all he wanted was the one thing not many of his clients wanted. Kissing. And right now, all rules about asking permission were forgotten, and he cradled Cam's face. "I'm going to kiss you until you can't breathe," he announced.

"Uh-huh," Cam murmured and went limp against the wall.

He was so gorgeous, and kissing this man would be worth every minute that Gabriel put into the work. He controlled the kiss, the pressure of the lips, the tongue, and the way he pulled back whenever Cam tried to make any kind of change to the kiss.

Meanwhile his hands moved down Cam's body, pausing at his nipples and gently caressing them, then harder, until he got the response he wanted, the groan of need in Cam's throat. At that point he pulled away, recalling how Cam wanted him to talk. He was a professional, and his ultimate goal was to get Cam off.

"You like that?" he asked, twisting his fingers a little, pulling at the nipple until it extended, moving the position of his hands so that he could concentrate on the teasing while the weight of his wrist and arms held Cam still. The position was awkward, but Cam rested his head against the wall, and his mouth was open, his lips wet from their kissing. He moaned low and deep, and Gabriel twisted that little bit harder, eliciting more moans. He replaced his fingers with his mouth and moved his hands to the band of Cam's sweats, hooking them and pushing them down.

"I'm going to hold you down and suck you until you're nearly there. You want me to do that?"

"God," Cam whimpered.

"Yeah, and then I'll stop, and I'll leave you on the edge. You like that?"

Cam reached wildly for Gabriel, for his head, his hair, before resting his hands on Gabriel's shoulders, clenching and unclenching on the muscles there. Then, refusing to yelp in pain as he slid to his knees, Gabriel was face-to-face with Cam's underwear, which he eased down smoothly. Cam was a nice size—a mouthful, a handful—and Gabriel's mouth watered at the thought of getting his lips wrapped around him.

He didn't wait. There was no talking. He wanted to take Cam over the edge right now, and he rolled on a condom before swallowing him. This wasn't finesse; this was need and right-fucking-now. Meanwhile, he gripped Cam's thighs and loved that Cam was trying to buck and couldn't. Cam's hands were on Gabriel's head, and as he came he let out a strangled moan.

Gabriel dealt with the condom, only realizing as he assisted Cam in easing down the wall that he was half hard from sucking him off. That wasn't right. He didn't get off on the work he did. It was a job, and him getting aroused in any way was not part of that.

Hell, he couldn't get aroused.

Only he was half hard, and the sight of Cam breathing heavily, his head back against the wall, his knees drawn up, had Gabriel thinking that somehow he'd lost control.

That scared him

"You close your eyes when you kiss." He said that to change the subject in his head. *I'm getting hard.*

"I do?" Cam said, like he hadn't considered that before. He reached out a hand to touch Gabriel's face. "Come here," he said.

Gabriel moved a little closer, his knees killing him. At least with Cam not being able to see, he didn't have to pretend he wasn't in pain.

"Can I?" Cam asked, and slid his hand up Gabriel's arm to his neck and then to his chin.

"Yeah," Gabriel murmured, and allowed Cam to trace his face.

"You're taller than me," Cam said. "I know that because Six told me, but also because when we kissed I had to tilt my head back. You're slim, but you have muscles in your arms. Do you work out?"

"Pushups and things," Gabriel said. "I'm not a gym

rat."

Cam smiled at him, that soft, cute smile, and continued his exploration. "You said you have Latino in you. How much?"

Gabriel shrugged, his usual response to that question.

"You need to use your words," Cam teased.

"A small bit, on my dad's side maybe."

Cam's fingers settled on his lips, tracing the shape of them, then moved up to his nose and across to his cheekbones. "You have a beautiful face," he murmured.

"Says the guy who can't see," Gabriel said without thought. "Sorry," he added.

"No offense taken," Cam said, and smiled even wider. "You have this beard going on," he added, and poked at it before running his fingers through the scruff. "Just at the sides and the chin. That's in fashion, I guess."

Gabriel recalled shaving off his thicker beard, leaving some, cutting his long hair short. "Yeah," he answered.

"I liked the feel of it on my cock," Cam said, bluntly and still with that infuriating smile.

"Good. I aim to please." He was trying for teasing, but Cam's smile slipped a little, and Gabriel needed it back. He wrapped his hand around Cam's soft cock and leaned in so his mouth was next to his ear. "I like the feel of your cock in my mouth."

"I'm not sixteen still," Cam said. "I can't go again."

So Gabriel showed him exactly how easy it was to get him hard again, only this time he stretched the time out, used every trick he knew, every dirty word that worked, until Cam was a mess of writhing need lying on the carpet.

"Gabriel, please."

Gabriel settled between Cam's legs, pain like knives

through his knees, and pushing the pain aside, he spread Cam's thighs and considered his next move. He lubed his finger and pressed it to Cam's hole as he licked the tip of his cock. He wasn't going to ask if that was okay, Cam wouldn't want to hear uncertainty, and the way he bucked up into Gabriel's mouth had him thinking he was doing something right. He added more lube, pressed harder, deeper, finding that elusive spot that he knew would send Cam wild. And all the time he was sucking and licking, and when Cam was coming he scrambled to hold on to any part of Gabriel he could reach until he fell back spent.

"You broke me," Cam mumbled behind the arm that flopped over his face. Then he held out a hand. "Help me up?"

"Hang on," Gabriel said, then used the wall and the nearby sofa to get to a standing position. His left knee buckled enough to steal his breath, and he closed his eyes, working his way through the pain.

"You okay?" Cam asked from the floor, rolling onto his side and then to his knees. Even in pain, Gabriel could appreciate the view, and then the muscles spasmed again.

"Yeah," And fuck, how much focus did it take even to form that simple word? He was far from fine. He hadn't been *fine* since Hank and Yuri had found him when he'd run and broken both his kneecaps with baseball bats. He was fucking lucky he could walk; pity his job had him on his knees so much. The spasm passed, but by this time Cam was up, pulling his sweats to his hips, so Gabriel wasn't there to help him stand. He picked up the Cowboys T-shirt and placed it deliberately into Cam's hand. Cam thanked him quietly and pulled it over his head.

"You like movies?" Cam asked, going into his kitchen

and confidently feeling his way around to fill the coffee machine with grounds. Was there anything Cam couldn't do?

"Some," Gabriel said. He couldn't recall the last film he'd seen—some Clint Eastwood boxing film, he thought, with a woman who died? All he remembered was that it had been boring, and sitting still that long had made him hurt all over. Still, the guy he was with had wanted a handjob in the movie theater, and a booking was a booking.

"I have a lot of everything," Cam said, and gestured to a large cupboard, "Help yourself."

Gabriel didn't move at first. He guessed it was impossible to fill the times with just sex, although he wouldn't mind getting Cam off a hundred times just to see his face.

He opened the door to the treasure trove, and so much color hit him that he blinked. Each DVD had a strip on the outside with more raised bumps, and it seemed like certain movies were grouped together. Flashy hero movies were in one spot, old black-and-white Laurel and Hardy comedies in another. The only group that looked random was ten cases on the top shelf alongside two trophies lying on their sides. He tilted his head to look at them, and they were for junior tennis, with Cam's name on them, another facet to this man's personality.

Up on this shelf was *The Shawshank Redemption*, nestled between *The Empire Strikes Back* and *Guardians of the Galaxy*.

"Why are these ones at the top separate?" he asked, and jumped when Cam spoke by his shoulder. He was losing it if Cam could get that close without him realizing.

"My favorite films. Well, at the moment. Pick one of those."

Gabriel reached in and pulled one out at random, and snorted at the choice. "*Armageddon*?" he asked. He'd seen it before on TV, but he wouldn't have expected it to be one of Cam's top ten films.

"Yeah, it was the last film I really watched," he said, and tapped his temples. "I don't even know why this one sticks out; it was full of clichés, but it stuck with me."

And now Gabriel felt like shit. He hadn't even thought about how a blind person watched a movie.

"We don't have to watch anything," he said quickly.

Cam handed him a coffee. "We can't have sex for the next few hours, much as I'd like to."

"You're paying me for sex."

"No, I'm paying you to stay with me on a boring off day. My manager has everything in hand, so it's just me and Gidget."

"But—"

"Anyway, I'd like to watch this with someone who isn't former Special Forces like Six. He spends whole movies telling me that a particular action sequence isn't feasible, or that a person wouldn't do this or that in a certain way. He's a real buzzkill."

They went to the sofa, Cam pushing the disc into the machine then sitting next to Gabriel.

Gabriel watched him carefully, saw the way he walked with a brush of his calf against the table, knowing when to turn, how to stand, when to sit. There wasn't much in the way of fumbling, like maybe he'd practiced this a lot. As soon as he sat down, Gidget jumped up next to him.

What about the practicalities of being blind? Who

walked Gidget? How did Cam learn a new room, or read people's reactions? Gabriel had so many questions, and he couldn't ask any of them.

Asking them would make this whole thing horribly intimate and real.

"Oh, wait." Cam pushed himself back off the sofa, Gidget padding after him. There was banging in the kitchen, then he walked back with an armful of chips. Gidget had a big chew bone. "Can't watch *Armageddon* without snacks," he announced, and dropped everything on the small table. "Help yourself. Not sure what's there."

"You have at least fifteen bags of Lays," Gabriel said, and counted the rest. "Yep, mostly that."

"Salt and vinegar. I love those. Pass me some."

Gabriel placed a bag in his lap. "You need me to open them?"

"Yeah," Cam said a little sadly. "Could you help me? I always worry I'll open them upside down and look really stupid."

Gabriel reached for the bag and there was a little tug-of-war

Cam huffed that small laugh of his. "Dude, I was joking, I can open chips. Jesus, I'm not totally incapable."

"Yeah, yeah, of course you can. I'm sorry, I didn't mean to imply…" Gabriel trailed off when he saw Cam's smiling expression. "Asshole," he added on the end.

"Sorry, couldn't help myself." Cam opened the bag and crunched the first handful of chips. "I went out with Adam once. He's the ex who… Yeah, never mind, he's the ex, which is the important thing. He took me out on our first date to this really cool restaurant, the ones where you eat in the dark."

"You eat in the dark?"

"Yep, it's all about sensory appreciation. Anyway, he freaked out, and whereas usually in restaurants people ask the guy I'm with what I want to eat—"

"You're joking."

"I promise you I'm not. It's as if I can't make decisions on my own. So Adam's freaking out, he can't see, he's panicking, and he doesn't like that it's me helping him. I should have known he was a waste of time."

The film started and they stopped talking to watch the first scenes, and before Gabriel knew it, the film had finished and they only had around two hours on the clock to go. He was feeling sleepy, warm from where Gidget had chosen to climb up between them, her head in Cam's lap, her ass and tail sprawled over Gabriel.

"Want to take Gidget for a walk with me?"

Gabriel nodded. "I'm still on the clock," he agreed.

He couldn't fail to notice Cam's subtle change in expression.

"And I'd like to," he added, hoping that would lessen the impact of reminding them both what he was doing there.

It seemed to work, and they walked with Gidget in the middle to a small park that nestled hidden behind the old hotel. They talked about everything and nothing, and Gabriel ignored the fact that his phone had vibrated in his pocket on several occasions. He knew it would be Stefan, but as soon as he got home a thousand or more richer, Stefan would be so damn happy.

When they arrived back at the hotel, there was an hour remaining, and when Gabriel left, dead on midnight, Cam was blissed out and making him promise to do this again.

Cam was clearly rich enough to afford it, and he added the client to his mental list. He liked being paid to watch films and talk actors and walk the dog.

Back at his apartment, he opened the door, and Stefan was waiting for him, leaning against the counter.

"I was worried," he said calmly.

"I had a job," Gabriel answered, and pulled out the envelope fat with hundred-dollar bills.

Stefan walked over and leaned past Gabriel to shut the door.

"Who for?" He took the money and opened the envelope, and Gabriel's chest puffed a little with pride.

"Cameron Stafford; paid for the whole afternoon and evening."

"You didn't call me."

"You said you were out all day."

"Still," Stefan patted Gabriel's cheek, "you should have called me, Angel. How can I look out for you if you don't let me know where you are?"

"I'm sorry," Gabriel said quickly. This could turn on a dime. Stefan could be happy because of the money, or get angry with him. Pride slid away from him and was replaced with fear, and he knew the moment when Stefan's calm control snapped.

And thankfully Gabriel didn't remain conscious for all of it.

CHAPTER 10

Cam shrugged on his suit jacket and clipped the leash to Gidget's harness. Today was D-day for hiring a new executive chef, and the last two interviews were part of his and the senior manager's responsibility. He had a hand in every major decision in this hotel; nothing happened without him knowing, and the things that could have slipped by, Six had a handle on.

"Ready?" Six asked from the door. "Esther is already down in the kitchens."

"Ready." They left the apartment and headed for the elevator. Cam heard the elevator ascend, tracing his hand over the ornate doors while he waited. The Stafford coat of arms, or at least what his grandparents had created as the coat of arms—a lion and a crown befitting Chicago aristocracy—was everywhere. From the stylized design he could trace on the elevator doors to the soft embossed logo on napkins and in the carpet. When he'd decided to take a leap of faith and run this place, his inheritance, himself, he'd gone with tradition. If a person stayed in any of the Stafford Hotels, they would see the same coat of arms, but his had the touch of luxury, and he was damn proud of the feel of it even if he couldn't see it.

The brand that he was integral to, despite the fact that no one had wanted him to be.

He'd worked damn hard to overcome everything, and he had Six to thank for a lot of it. That gave him pause, and he reached out to touch Six on the arm.

"Thank you," he said. "I never say it enough."

"What for?" Six asked.

"For everything," Cam said expansively.

The soft *ding* of the approaching car made him jump enough to stop the conversation, and when the door opened he made to step in, only for Six to grab his arm and yank him back.

"Fuck," Six cursed. "Jesus," he added with feeling.

"What?" Cam snapped. "What is it?"

"Cam?"

That was Gabriel's rough voice; he'd know it anywhere. "Can you help me?"

"Out of the way," Six snapped, and shoved at Cam a little before pushing past him. "What the fuck happened to you?"

"I just need to borrow some money."

"Fuck off, he's not giving you money."

"I'll pay him back. Please, I wouldn't ask—"

"I said no. Get out of here. Take yourself to a hospital, or a street corner, I don't fucking care, but get out of this hotel."

Cam couldn't follow this. Gabriel sounded...wrong...and Six was shouting and saying things for Cam that he wouldn't have said at all.

"Stop!" Cam snapped. The doors of the elevator tried to shut, but he was in the way and they moved back. "Someone tell me what's happening."

"What's happening is this street trash needs to get his ass out of the hotel."

"I just need to borrow enough to get some help," Gabriel pleaded.

They spoke at the same time.

And then there was a thump and everything went

quiet. Had Six hit Gabriel? Gidget was agitated, whining at his side.

"Six!"

"Move back, Cam," Six ordered, and then there was more grunting, and noises that Cam couldn't make out. "In your apartment. It's Gabriel, he looks like he's been mugged. Call 9-1-1."

"No…" Gabriel said on a groan. "Jus' need money."

Cam pulled the door shut behind him. "Talk to me, Six."

"He's bleeding, not sure from where. Hold still, fuck's sake."

"Get off me."

"Whatever," Six snapped, and there was another flurry of activity, and Cam focused in on the sounds and scents. Antiseptic, soft curse words, the coppery smell of blood, and he stepped forward into a spot he knew was between Gabriel and Six, holding up his hands, Gidget right close to him.

"Six, give me a report."

"One cut above the eye, bleeding through a bandage that looks like a child stuck it there. He's bent over a bit, I'm thinking bruised ribs, a lot of marks on his neck, I can't make them out. We need to call the police."

"No police." That came from Gabriel.

"Jesus, he's spitting blood now." Six yanked at Cam, who nearly toppled and righted himself with a hand to Six's chest.

"Stop, Six. Gabriel, talk to me."

"I just need to borrow some money." There was the sound of something, material, Gidget moving, and then some soft words. "I'll do anything." Gabriel's voice had moved. It was lower. Gabriel was lower.

"Six?" Cam asked a little desperately.

"He's on his fucking knees in front of you."

"What happened?" Cam asked. He wanted to see this; he desperately wanted to be in control of what was happening here.

"Probably took some other guy's corner," Six grumbled.

"I didn't. Please, Cam, I'll pay it back."

"What do you need it for?"

"A bus, a cab, anything."

Cam followed his instincts and went to a crouch, reaching for something to balance on, finding Gabriel's shoulder. Gabriel hissed at the touch. "How much do you need?"

"I have an address I need to get to," Gabriel said, and his voice was thick with tears. He coughed, and the motion moved Cam's hand.

"Do you need a hospital?" he asked, but Gabriel stayed quiet. "Six, does he need a hospital?"

Six was suspiciously quiet as well.

"Someone fucking talk to me," he snapped, and had to place a reassuring hand against Gidget, who whined again. He knew how Gidget felt; he didn't understand what was going on either.

"Can you breathe?" Six asked, his voice calmer but still firm. He moved past Cam and lifted Cam's hand from Gabriel. "Does it hurt when you breathe?"

"No."

"Relax, I'm not going to hurt you," Six snapped when Gabriel hissed.

Cam had to stay calm; Six was a trained professional

and had to have seen firsthand his share of battlefield medicine. Right?

"When did this happen?" he asked, and Gabriel mumbled something that sounded like one a.m. After he'd left here last night? On his way home? Six ran through a whole gamut of questions and Cam stood up, a head rush making him sway a little. He listened to the answers. Yes, he'd lost consciousness. No, he hadn't been sick. He didn't have a headache, and please could he just have some money.

"You need to see a doctor to be sure," Six said in conclusion.

"After I get where I need to be," Gabriel snapped back.

Cam made a decision. "Six, get the car; we'll take him where he needs to go." He held up a hand, because he knew Six would hate that, and that Gabriel wouldn't be happy. He didn't have to know Gabriel well to assume that something huge enough had happened that he wouldn't trust anyone.

The chaos around him made his head spin, but at least neither man said anything. God knew what kind of expressions they had on their faces right then, or what sort of death glare Six was giving Gabriel. The door slammed, and Cam crossed to the desk phone, pressing for reception and connecting to the hotel manager. He explained that he wouldn't be at the meeting. Finally, he was back with Gabriel, who as far as he knew was still on his knees.

"What happened, Gabriel?" he asked gently.

Gabriel said nothing, but he did move, and his soft exhalation of pain cut Cam to the core.

"He didn't like that I didn't tell him where I was. I let

him down."

"Who?"

"Stefan. He's my…" Silence.

Pimp? Friend? Lover? None of those labels sat well with Cam.

"He's your what?"

"What am I doing? I can't leave here. I need to go back to him. I don't know what I was thinking… I can't…"

Cam crossed to the door and stood with his back to it. "You're not going back to the person who hurt you."

Gabriel was pulling at him, but his movements were weak, and that didn't bode well. "Let me out. I have to go back to him."

Six knocked and said it was him, and Cam eased away from the door, keeping a hand on Gabriel's arm.

"I'm taking you somewhere, anywhere but back to him."

And Gabriel sagged against him, his fight gone. But, only when they were in the car did Cam relax a little.

"Where are we going?" Six asked.

"Legacy Ranch. It's part of the Double D," Gabriel murmured.

"I want it on record that I insisted we take Gabriel to the police."

"Noted," Cam agreed. "Is that the Campbell-Hayes place?"

"Kyle," Gabriel murmured. "And Mistry."

Cam felt a weight leaning against him, then the soft sounds of breathing. Had Gabriel fallen asleep on him, or was he unconscious? Whatever it was, Cam was worried, and he shook his shoulder a little.

"Sorry," Gabriel murmured. Not unconscious or asleep, then, in which case he'd been looking for comfort; that Cam could do.

He searched for Gabriel's hand and held it firmly, then tugged so Gabriel was leaning on him again.

"No need to be sorry," he began, then thought he'd try one more time. "A doctor seems like a good idea."

"No."

"Or the cops?"

"No. Just Kyle."

Whoever this Kyle was, he hoped that meeting the man would make sense of what had started as an ordinary day.

The Double D Ranch wasn't that far out of Dallas, but enough of a distance for Gabriel to fall into a fitful sleep.

"I don't like this," Six said from up front. "This isn't something I signed up for. I'm supposed to protect you, look out for you, not get pulled into crazy hooker shit."

"Six—"

"Don't, Cam, just don't. This is the worst fucking idea I've ever been party to."

There was a sign a few hundred yards past the main Double D ranch pointing a visitor to something called Legacy, which seemed to fit what Gabriel was looking for. Six clearly thought the same thing, turning off and parking up at the far end of the road. Cam could see a structure through the tinted windows—a long, low-slung building and some figures standing outside.

"Gabriel?" He gently shook the sleeping man, who curled closer to Cam then seemed to come awake in an instant.

He let out a moan of pain, but that was it, and it didn't last long. "We're here?" he asked. He gripped Cam's hand.

"Yeah. You want to get out?"

"Not really," Gabriel murmured, then he pulled himself away from Cam. "But I need to."

Six opened the door on Cam's side and Gidget jumped down. Cam followed her, his hand on the handle of the harness and Gabriel following.

"You don't have to stay," Gabriel said. But there was something in his tone that screamed fear, and right now, Cam didn't want Gabriel being scared.

"I won't go until I know you're okay." Cam wanted to find out who Kyle was, what he meant to Gabriel, and why the hell any kind of connection made Cam feel a twinge of jealousy.

For a hooker, for god's sake.

Gabriel took his hand and began to walk, and he led Cam with him.

And suddenly Gabriel wasn't a hooker that had crashed into Cam's dark world and turned it on its head.

Gabriel was a friend.

CHAPTER 11

Gabriel hurt. From the top of his head, which he knew had contacted the wall, to the little finger of his left hand, which he thought could be broken. Stefan hadn't stopped, he'd been furious, and when Gabriel had come around, woken from whatever safe place his mind had escaped to, he'd known he had to leave until Stefan calmed down.

Only he hadn't known where to go.

He'd disappointed Stefan, and he'd needed to go somewhere and make himself better, and all he'd been able to think had been that Kyle had a safe place for him. Legacy Ranch. They would help him, and he could go home and Stefan wouldn't see him all broken up.

There were two men outside the main structure, one tall and rangy and blond, the other shorter with dark hair, and as they got closer Gabriel could make out a third man, partially obscured. He recognized that third man. Kyle. He wasn't going to forget any details about the trial, and he certainly recalled stoic Kyle.

It was Kyle who stepped forward, an expression of puzzlement on his face, but it was Tall and Blond who spoke.

"Cam?" he said.

"Riley," Cam said from Gabriel's side.

"Is everything okay?"

Then realization dawned on Kyle's face and he hurried to the other side of Gabriel, which was a good thing, because all the energy was leaving Gabriel in one big rush. Part of him didn't want to let Cam go, but Cam was actually handing him to Kyle, and why wouldn't he? Gabriel was just a mess of problems and issues and a tangled knot of pain.

Kyle didn't say anything, just supported Gabriel and helped him inside the large structure, taking him through a kitchen and to a room at the back.

"Can I see?" he asked carefully, and Gabriel knew what he meant. Slowly, he eased off his shirt, the pain in his left shoulder hindering him. Kyle didn't move to assist, and that was okay; he could do this himself.

Until he couldn't.

"Can you help?" he asked, and Kyle moved quickly to tug the shirt off and help Gabriel with his jeans. In boxers, he deliberately turned around so Kyle could see his back, then half turned to expose the bruising on his side, and finally faced him so that every mark on his body was obvious.

This was mechanical, and he was beyond caring what another victim like Kyle was thinking. He was sure Kyle had suffered the same way he had at the hands of Hank. Why would anything he saw now be a shock?

But Kyle's eyes were wet, like he was holding back tears and it wasn't quite working.

"I just need somewhere to stay for a few days," Gabriel said, shoulders back, however much that hurt. "I don't want any questions, or a doctor, or any shit like that."

Kyle nodded. "The man who helped you here—"

"Is no one."

Kyle crossed his arms over his chest and looked concerned. "Is he the one hurting you?"

Just the idea of Cam hurting anyone with hands or

words made Gabriel snort a laugh, which hurt like a freaking bitch.

"No, he's nothing to do with me," Gabriel lied.

Kyle narrowed his eyes. "He looked pretty invested in your welfare," he said.

"He's a fucking mark, okay? He's nothing to me. Tell him to go."

Thankfully, a knock at the door stopped the discussion about Cam, and also, abruptly, shame coiled inside Gabriel. He didn't want anyone else to see him nearly naked, with every mark on his body on show. He didn't know how to voice that, though.

"Gabriel? It's me," Cam called through the door.

Kyle looked at him expectantly, but Gabriel closed his eyes and shook his head. He didn't want to see Cam, couldn't handle questions. It was bad enough he'd fallen asleep on the man's shoulder.

His head hurt. Stefan should be here; he'd be able to calm the pain in his thoughts, and kiss every bruise like it was a badge of honor. Cam was just the mark he'd used to get here; fucking man wouldn't let himself get sucked off for money to get a cab, no, he'd insisted on bringing him here.

What if Stefan found out?

That didn't bear thinking about. He'd be so disappointed in Gabriel. The pain in his body seemed to reach right into his heart and his defiant stance slumped a little. Kyle was still standing there watching and likely had his own opinions about what was happening in Gabriel's head.

"Don't let him in," Gabriel said.

Kyle nodded. "Do you want me to call the police?"

For Cam? Was that what Kyle meant? Did he not believe that Cam had nothing to do with this? That Cam had rescued him? Or at least badgered him into accompanying him here. That wasn't so much rescuing as getting into the middle of things he shouldn't be involved with.

If Stefan found out…

"No. Just tell him to go."

He was asking a lot of Kyle to have to deal with the man outside the door, but he didn't want to see Cam.

"I'll be right back," Kyle murmured, then slipped out the door. Gabriel could hear the low rumble of voices, but the doors were thick wood, and anyway he didn't want to hear Cam's do-gooder shit right now.

For the longest time he sat on the bed, looking out the window. Beyond the glass and to the left were some stables, and every so often he caught a glimpse of movement inside. His eyesight was a little blurry, but he was tired, right? He opened and closed his eyes a few times, but the blurriness was morphing into a prism in his eyes. So he closed them completely and lay back on the bed, but the pain chased him even in the darkness.

"Gabriel?" a voice asked him, but he didn't know who it was. He wanted to open his eyes, but that hurt.

"I think we need… doctor…"

I can't afford a doctor. I'll be okay.

"Gabriel, can you hear me?"

Go away.

"Gabriel? My name is Clair…"

"I'll stay with him."

"You need to wake him…"

Light woke him, not bright like the ones in the night, or day, or whenever they'd insisted on shining something into his eyes. This was a softer light, and the pain in his head had subsided. He needed to get up; sickness roiled inside him, and he leaned on his side groaning, unable to stop the vomit that forced itself up out of him.

Someone held him, and he half opened his eyes, shutting them immediately. He didn't know who was holding him, didn't recognize him at all. Someone had their hands on him, and he hadn't agreed to that. He struggled to get away, but nothing worked, and every molecule of him hurt.

That same person who was supporting him gave him ice chips and helped him to lay back.

Next time he opened his eyes, it was Kyle sitting next to the bed, leaning back in the chair, his fingers laced and his hands on his belly. His hat was tipped forward, hiding his eyes, and he looked completely at peace. There was water on the side, and Gabriel reached for it, but Kyle was there helping when he couldn't quite make contact with the glass.

He allowed Kyle's help, then shuffled back and away.

"How are you feeling?" Kyle asked, concern in his green eyes.

Gabriel blinked. He felt okay, his eyesight wasn't blurry, and the pain was at a manageable level, or at least at a level he could handle from experience.

He needed his clothes, and to get out of there. Stefan would be wondering where he was.

"Did he call?" Gabriel asked a little desperately.

"We didn't find a phone on you."

Fear gripped Gabriel, then he recalled what he'd done

with it and he groaned out loud. His only lifeline to Stefan was at the bottom of the river. Why had he done that? He was so fucking stupid. It wasn't like Stefan had meant to take things so far this time, and he'd had every right to be angry after all the time he'd looked after Gabriel. He pushed himself to sit up, moving to set his feet on the floor.

"What do you need?" Kyle asked immediately, and reached for him.

"My clothes," Gabriel said, peering down at the floor where he seemed to recall his clothes had dropped.

"You need to stay in bed for a while."

"No, I need to get back home."

"The doctor says you should stay here."

Horrified, Gabriel looked right at Kyle. "I can't afford a fucking doctor. I told you no fucking doctor." How much of his saved money was that going to take? He'd been so close to his target, and every cent would probably be gone once he saw the invoice.

"Legacy has medical insurance."

"I'll still owe someone."

"No. You won't."

"I need to go." He used the bed as a point to lean on as he tried to stand. Kyle held his arm, to support him or stop him, Gabriel didn't know. All he did know was the panic that gripped him and made it hard to breathe. "Stefan will kill me," he blurted.

Kyle didn't let go, but his hold gentled even more. "Does he know where you are?"

Kyle hadn't asked who Stefan was, or why Gabriel was so desperate to get home, but he'd asked the one question that sounded more like an accusation. Gabriel pulled his arm free of Kyle's hold.

"No," Gabriel said, "he doesn't know, and he'll be frantic."

"This is your friend? A friend, I mean, not someone you're scared of."

"I'm not scared of Stefan. He looks after me."

Something poked at the back of his thoughts, an insistent press that called him a liar. He wasn't scared of Stefan, he was scared of disappointing the man who'd taken him in. That was all.

"Is he abusing you?" Kyle asked, oh-so-fucking gently.

"What?" Gabriel's temper began to grow. "No."

"Okay."

And that was it. Didn't matter about his headache, his temper blew. "He found me on a street corner and he took me in." Gabriel shoved Kyle, and his voice was rising in volume to match his need to defend Stefan. "He paid for me, looked after me, and I was the one who fucked up, okay? I didn't tell him I took a booking with someone he'd warned me against. Okay? He told me he needed to know if I went back to Cam, and I didn't tell him. No wonder he was fucking pissed."

Kyle didn't retaliate even as Gabriel shoved him back against the wall. He didn't look scared. Hell, why would he be scared? Gabriel was a pathetic mess without Stefan looking out for him.

And the tears started. He couldn't stop them as they spilled out of his eyes and trickled down his face, and all that time Kyle simply looked at him with a steady gaze that didn't hold any sympathy, only a hell of a lot of understanding.

"What do you know?" Gabriel shouted in his face, and shoved him so hard that Kyle let out an exhalation of shock. Still he didn't fight back, didn't defend himself, just looked at Gabriel all calm and tight with control. "You found this place, and your fucking boyfriend, and horses, and you didn't need help from anyone, so what do you know about how Stefan helps me? Huh?"

He shoved Kyle again, and the tears still flowed.

"It's okay," Kyle murmured. "I know."

If it was possible, temper went up another notch in Gabriel's pained head. "You don't know fuck all. You were there for such a short time; I was there years. You get that, right?"

Somehow the conversation had become a very different thing, not about Stefan but about what had happened back at the Bar Five, about Hank Castille and Yuri Fensin.

"I should have said something," Kyle said, and he sounded wretched. Finally there was something in those green eyes—regret, maybe?

"And Stefan, he took me, and he helped me, and he made me so I can make my way forward."

"He didn't," Kyle said firmly. "He's hurting you."

"You don't know a fucking thing! You don't care!" That was it; he curled his fists and wanted to hit Kyle, but someone was there, holding him back, strong but not hurting him as he attempted to wriggle free. Someone was talking to him, right in his ear, whispering, telling him everything was going to be okay.

And even though nothing would ever be okay, Gabriel had no choice but to relax.

"That's okay," the voice continued. "Let's get you

dressed and get some food in you."

"Hmmm," Gabriel murmured, suddenly devoid of any strength or emotion.

Kyle helped him dress in soft sweats and a loose T, then showed him the bathroom.

For the longest time, Gabriel stared at himself in the mirror. His face was bruised, and he had a cut with small butterfly bandages on it. He hoped it wouldn't scar; clients didn't want to see scars and blemishes on what they'd bought.

"You okay in there?" Kyle called in.

Gabriel stepped out, and Kyle guided him to a large wooden table in the kitchen. It was daylight. Had he slept around the clock, or was it the same day? Somehow he'd expected Cam to be sitting there, but the only movement was from a dark-haired man; he must be the one who'd held him.

"I need to check on the horses," Kyle said, and leaned over to press a kiss to the other guy's lips. Then he left, but not before he'd looked at Gabriel and then back at the man with the spatula. "Call me if you need me."

The dark-haired man scooped eggs onto a plate and put it, along with a plate of crispy bacon and toast, onto the table.

"I'm Jason," he said. Jason had impossibly dark eyes and a ready smile, and he pushed a plate over to Gabriel. "No one can resist bacon," he added, and handed over cutlery as well. "Would you like juice? I'd offer coffee, but the doc said you might want to avoid stimulants for the next few days. Having said that, do you know if there's anything in orange juice? Who knows these days, when it's out of a box?"

Gabriel just blinked at Jason and tried to filter through all the words. "Juice is fine," he finally said. He was hungry, and Stefan would want him to eat—he'd be pleased if Gabriel was looking after himself.

He picked at some eggs and ate a strip of bacon, then swallowed some headache pills with the sweet orange juice. He hadn't realized how hungry he was.

"So, I sucked off guys in the park for money," Jason announced after he'd chewed an entire slice of crispy bacon that he'd folded to put in his mouth in one piece.

"Sorry?" Gabriel had only caught the end of it properly.

"I did it for money," he said. "There's no shame in doing what you need to do to live."

Gabriel looked at Jason, at the smile and the compassion, and shook his head. "I suck men off to earn money. It's my career and I'm good at it. There's no shame in sex as a career."

Jason grinned at him, a wide smile that reached his eyes. "Yeah, you do what you have to."

"I didn't have to do it. I had a choice." Stefan had said he didn't need to have sex for money if he could find another way to pay the rent.

I had a choice.

"Then you're one of the lucky ones. I was too young to get hired anywhere. I didn't have a choice. It was either blowjobs or back into the system, and I was done with that. I'm here and safe and with Kyle. You met him—he's the strong, silent one who sat by your bed all night."

All night implied it was now the next day. Which meant it had been two days since he'd seen Stefan.

"Yeah, you were pretty out of it, but the doc kept an

eye on you, and we took it in turns sitting with you, although Kyle took the bulk of it. He's a good guy, you know, and he's watched you now for four days."

"A good guy wouldn't take my clothes and stop me from leaving," Gabriel snapped. And this was day four? Jesus, he needed to get hold of Stefan.

"You can go if you want, anytime. I can call you a cab."

"Yeah, do that."

Jason fished a phone out of his pocket and dialed a number. "I need a cab... Legacy Ranch... Dallas... Thanks." He ended the call and looked expectantly at Gabriel. "An hour," he announced.

"An hour? What the hell?"

"We're in the middle of nowhere, dude," Jason said with another one of his smiles. "So chill, and we'll make sure you get taken care of."

Gabriel relaxed a little. They weren't making him stay, and he could get in the cab and go back to Stefan and explain this away somehow. Four days missing and a doctor's tab wasn't going to be easy to explain, but he'd do it. Stefan would likely be angry, but he could handle that.

The main door opened and daylight flooded the inside of the kitchen. A woman stepped in, and for a second he couldn't make out her features with the sun behind her, and his chest constricted. She was small, like his mom, her hair long and loose, like his mom's.

Only after she shut the door did his breathing ease. Of course it wasn't his mom; she'd died a long time ago.

"Hi, my name is Clair," she said, and held out a hand to Gabriel. He took it, because he had manners, then wriggled a little in his chair as she sat down in front of him. Jason gave her coffee, offered breakfast, which she declined, then grabbed a to-go cup, made his excuses and left.

That had to be the most poorly executed maneuver he'd ever seen. Clearly this woman was there to meet him.

"What?" he asked suspiciously when she said nothing at first.

She placed her cell in the middle of the table. "Would you like to phone someone?" she asked. "Feel free to use it—my phone plan covers all kinds of eventualities."

Gabriel's fingers twitched with the need to connect to Stefan, but he didn't touch the phone and couldn't work out why.

"Thank you," he said, politely. He looked at the woman more closely. She didn't look much older than him.

"I wanted to come in and talk to you, see how you're doing."

"What are you? A shrink? I don't need to talk to a fucking shrink." He winced as he said that. His mom would have had a fit if she'd heard him cussing like that in front of a lady.

"I'm not really one of those, just a friend of Legacy Ranch," she said after a moment's pause. "I guess I'm the one who makes sure you want to be here and helps you to decide what you want to do next."

He'd come across this sort of do-gooder before, mostly attached to one religion or another, horrified that a boy wasn't willing to turn to *their* particular deity, or some such shit they were peddling. Whoever God was, he'd taken Gabriel's mom and left Gabriel at the Bar Five to get hurt.

"I want to go home. Jason called a cab for me."

"Wonderful," Clair said, and reached for her coffee. "Kyle said you were in an accident?"

Gabriel tensed. An accident? Was that an attempt to get him to tell her what had really happened? Was she implying it hadn't been an accident? Stefan didn't mean to get so angry, it just happened.

Then why did you go to Cam? Why did you run here?

"No, I pissed off my friend and he hit me." He was aiming for shock value, and waited for the gasp of horror. There was nothing. She nodded and took another sip of her coffee.

"How did you piss him off?"

"Fuck off if I'm talking about this with you."

"It's fine, you don't have to, just seems to me if he's a friend he wouldn't be hitting you, is all. Is he actually a boyfriend?"

Gabriel didn't want to admit that at the start that was exactly what he'd thought Stefan was to him. The older man had shown him such open affection, getting him tested, feeding him, buying him clothes. That had been what Gabriel's definition of great kindness was, and sue him if he hadn't fallen just a little bit in love with him.

Completely inappropriate, as Stefan had explained when Gabriel told him. They had a relationship based on sex, and Gabriel should be satisfied with that.

And mostly Gabriel was.

They weren't married or anything like that. If they were, like Sophie and Mitchell, then that would be abuse, because when you're married you should be in love and everything should be fair.

"Just a friend. A person like me doesn't have boyfriends, or even deserve them."

"Gabriel—"

"I might as well not be here anymore," he said, rambling without purpose. What *was* the point of any of this? What was the purpose in fighting?

"Are you having suicidal thoughts, Gabriel?"

"No," he lied. It wouldn't be suicide; it would just be sleeping and not having the mess in his head. That was all.

Shakily, he reached for the phone, waiting for her to snatch it back, and pressed the screen to see the time. Eleven fifteen, and the taxi had been called about ten minutes ago, he guessed, or thereabouts at least.

"I need some air," he announced, and stood up, gripping the table when he had a rush of blood to the head.

She didn't fuss over him or reach for him, but he made it to the door still feeling like the hounds of hell were at his heels.

The day was warm, the sun high, and the scents of the ranch hit him worse than they had yesterday. An attack of animals, and straw, and the sounds of horses, and someone looking at him. Kyle again.

"Hey," Kyle said. "Want to meet Mistry? This way."

Blindly, not sure what the hell he was doing, he followed Kyle to the barns, the itch of memories just out of reach. The last time he'd been on a ranch, he'd been left to bleed out, he'd been left to die, and he couldn't walk, and the pain… God, the pain. He kept walking now, just as he had then, only this time he was heading right for the scents and noises of things he'd sworn to forget.

"This is Mistry," Kyle said, and crooned at the big quarter horse. He held out a handful of feed, and Mistry snuffled at the hand, puffing air, and it was all Gabriel could do not to run. "We had a run-in with the guy who said he owned Mistry again yesterday. I had to get Jack down here."

Interested despite himself, Gabriel looked expectantly at Kyle. "What happened?"

"He'd brought a trailer and papers, just like we'd said he should, but they didn't look right to me, and then Jack arrived, and I've never seen anything like it." Kyle shook his head and scratched Mistry's face, smiling when Mistry butted his hand for more food. "Jack stood between the guy and Mistry and refused to move. Said that this stranger should call the cops, because no one was messing with a Campbell-Hayes horse. I swear the guy went pale, but he was blustering about ownership rights, and Jack listed off the fact that the horse had been abandoned, and was underweight, and hell, an entire list of issues."

"I bet Jack laid him out."

Kyle looked at him with an unreadable expression, then his lips thinned. "Jack doesn't go around hitting people, he just has this way about him, and the guy backed off. Took his trailer and left the ranch."

Silence, and cautiously Gabriel reached out and stroked the wiry mane, twisting his fingers into it a little. Sense memory of time with horses consumed his thoughts, and for the longest time he stood there and soaked it all in. The closest he got to horses in the city was the mounted police that he saw sometimes. Mistry nuzzled him, and for the first time in a long time, at least that he could recall, Gabriel smiled. Seemed to him the last time he'd smiled had been thinking Stefan would be proud of the money he'd brought in from Cam.

"Do you ride?"

The question was loaded—not so much do you ride, more have you ridden since you left the Bar Five.

"Not anymore," he said truthfully.

"If you want to ride today, we could arrange something. Doc said to take it easy, but…"

"No, my cab will be here soon."

Kyle nodded. "Jason said you'd asked him to call one."

"I need to go home," Gabriel said quickly. "To go back," he corrected himself. Home had been a cabin on Bar Five land with his mom—home wasn't with Stefan, not really. Home was warm and safe.

I'm safe with Stefan. He doesn't let anyone else hurt me.

He hunched over at the pain in chest as his breath hitched, and he was fucking crying again, for god's sake. Kyle placed a hand on his arm, then slowly drew him closer until Gabriel was leaning into him and crying. He didn't know how long he stood there, but Kyle knew what it had been like; he'd been hurt by those men at the Bar Five, he'd given evidence at the same trial.

They had an association. A horrible, vicious, unacceptable connection, but it would always be there.

"You can stay," Kyle said. "There's work here, your own room, and you'll be safe."

Indecision gripped Gabriel, and that was the first time since Stefan had helped him that he'd doubted his path in life.

"I can't," he said, his voice a little broken even to his own ears.

"Don't go back," Kyle murmured. They were still

hugging, and Gabriel was still crying, silently. "You don't have to go back."

Gabriel eased himself away. "Stefan will find me..." he began.

"We'll protect you, but it won't be easy..."

Gabriel's heart shattered at that moment. He didn't deserve this, he wasn't ready for this, and he knew what it was that he couldn't make Kyle understand.

"I don't deserve for it to be easy," he said. He stopped crying then, because what was the point in any of it?

When the taxi arrived, they didn't stop him leaving. They didn't touch him. Instead, Kyle and Jason stood hand in hand and watched him go. Legacy was covering the cost of it, and thank fuck for that, because he had nothing on him except the keys to Stefan's place.

Not even his phone, which he'd thrown in the river.

There was no sign of Clair, whoever the hell she was, and the last view Gabriel had from the side of the car was of Mistry, turned out in the field and watching him leave.

Or was that just him being fanciful?

The cab dropped him outside Stefan's building, and Gabriel didn't hesitate or think it through. He climbed the stairs and let himself in. Stefan was there, sitting at the table, nursing a coffee, but he scrambled to stand. In an instant, Gabriel was in his arms, and Stefan hugged him close.

"I'm sorry," he said. "So sorry."

And for Gabriel, that was enough.

CHAPTER 12

"He left," Riley said, and the words sent a shiver of fear down Cam's spine. He'd asked his friend to phone him with updates, but this was the first real one that Riley could give him that wasn't "he's sleeping" or "he's hurting".

"What do you mean?"

"He just left—wanted a cab called, and we couldn't exactly stop him."

"Where did he go?"

Riley repeated the address the cab had been given, and Cam's heart sank. Back to the apartment with the man who'd hurt him.

"Thank you anyway," Cam said, and waited for Riley to say something, like a goodbye. Instead Riley began to talk about things that made Cam feel far from comfortable.

"If you need our help, or anything at all, to get him away from the life he's in at the moment, then you know where we are. Jack and I, we don't judge in any way for what a man has been through in his life. And Cam, I have to say, Gabriel looked hollow-eyed when he was here, like he didn't have any passion for life left in him. Like he wanted to die."

"What?"

"He said some things to Clair... She's someone who works at the ranch with some of the visitors who need some help. She's a friend of Steve Murray. You know him."

Cam was impatient to get to the point of this

conversation, and decided that direct was for the best. "Are you saying he didn't want to be alive anymore? Are we…" He couldn't even voice the words. Concern for Gabriel was twisting itself inside him, and he wasn't entirely sure why. Of course, there was the fact he was a human being who was in trouble, or at least stuck somewhere awful, but this was a hooker he'd bought for two nights.

I shouldn't care this much.

However, he'd be the first person to admit that he might care too much.

"I need you to book Gabriel again," Cam told Six.

"No."

"Six—"

"This is ridiculous. That man is nothing but trouble. He had every chance to get out of that life, and he turned it down. He's damaged goods, and it's up to me to see things that you can't. So no, I won't book him."

Cam brushed past Six, walking straight into the table and cursing to himself, but at least he'd found the table.

"What are you doing?"

"Finding the number, because you have to book him for me, and my phone is in my room," he said, and ran his hand over the table, coming to a dead stop next to a mug and tracing his way around it.

"Jesus, Cam—"

"I need to speak to Gabriel. I have to stop him from doing anything stupid."

He ran his hand across the table, not sure what he was looking for—a Rolodex or something? Did people even have those anymore?

A strong hand clasped his and he tried to shake it off. Stepping back, he tangled Gidget's harness up in his legs, and the next thing he knew he'd stepped on her. She yelped.

"Stop, Cam. Just stop."

Cam left his hand fly, connecting with part of Six, then falling back to slide down the wall and sit on the floor, Gidget pressing into him.

"Shit," Cam muttered, burying his face in her soft fur and holding tight. "I hurt Gidget."

"She's okay," Six said from close by, clearly kneeling next to Cam, or maybe crouching. Who the hell knew? "Tell me what's going on."

Cam knocked his head back against the wall. He was going to sound stupid, talking about a weird-ass connection to a man he'd only spent two evenings with.

"I feel something for him, okay? Compassion, sorrow…fuck knows what it is, but I need to do something."

"I'll get him here."

"For the whole night. I'll pay what it takes."

"That makes no fucking sense, Cam—"

"No, you see, if I make a standing booking, every week, one night, and I pay a lot… I mean, I have the money—I can pay what the hell I want, can't I?"

"You're not making sense."

"I am. If he has a booking, then maybe…" His voice broke, and Gidget butted him with her cold nose.

"Maybe what?"

"Maybe he won't kill himself."

Silence.

Then he felt Six sit next to him, his back against the

same wall, his voice thick with emotion. "Jesus, Cam."

And all Cam could say over and over was two simple words. "I know. I know."

Cam was nervous the first time. He wasn't even sure that Gabriel would take the booking, or this Stefan guy that Six booked through. As soon as Six had organized the booking, Cam started to worry. What if Gabriel had told his pimp that it had been Cam he'd turned to in order to get out of the city and to Legacy Ranch? Just booking him again could have put him in danger.

The knock was loud, and Cam walked to the door to let Gabriel in. He opened it wide and stood to one side, and he knew it was Gabriel there. Six had told him he was on the way up, and there was Gabriel's unique scent.

"Gabriel," Cam murmured.

Gabriel came in and Cam shut the door.

"This isn't good," Gabriel said.

Cam wasn't even going there. "How are you?"

"What?"

"It's polite. I'm being polite. I want to know how you are. How have you been? How is your head?"

Did Stefan hurt you? Are you covered in bruises? Have you bled for the man you ran back to?

"It's all good. Where do you want me?"

"What film do you want to watch?"

"You didn't pay me to watch films."

"I did. Didn't Six say that?"

Gabriel didn't answer, but the next thing Cam knew, he was being pressed back against the wall, and Gabriel had his hands down his pants.

"We need to talk," Cam said, and tried to push Gabriel

away, but after a few seconds, Gabriel's teeth scraping Cam's throat and his hand moving rhythmically on his cock, he realized he didn't want to talk at all. He wanted more of this. Didn't matter if it was wrong, if he'd booked Gabriel so they could talk—it felt too good right now.

Gabriel pushed down Cam's pants and underwear and went to his knees, rolled on a condom and sucked Cam to the point where he was close, then he backed away.

"What do you want?" he asked.

Was there more to that question? Was it something deeper than just how Cam wanted to come?

"I want to talk," Cam said, his orgasm fading, and suddenly the absurdity of standing there half naked with Gabriel somewhere on the floor, probably looking up at him, was enough for him to yank up his underwear, then his pants, and button them.

"You didn't pay me to talk."

"Jesus, Gabriel, I paid you to do whatever the hell I want for the next four hours."

"Okay," Gabriel said after a short pause, and then there was the noise of him standing up, and the cracking of his knees was obvious in the otherwise silent room.

"Don't go to your knees again," Cam said, realizing it sounded more like an order than a request.

"Yes, sir," Gabriel murmured.

"Choose a film; I'll get snacks. You want Sprite?" He didn't wait for an answer, just navigated his way to the kitchen and pulled out all the snacks he could feel, along with two bottles in the fridge—Sprite for Gabriel, water for him. He stuck his head in the fridge, the cold welcome on his flushed face. God, he'd wanted to come so bad, but that wasn't what this was for.

They settled in front of Gabriel's choice, *Lethal Weapon*, and sat for the entire film in silence. He felt his watch—he still had at least two hours left.

"I'll get some food sent up," he announced, and reached for the in-house phone on the table next to the sofa. Gidget grumbled but moved out of the way, and finally Cam was connected to the kitchen. He ordered whatever was in season and a bottle of whichever wine matched the food.

He didn't bother asking Gabriel, because he expected him to say that Cam wasn't paying him to make dinner choices.

"I'm setting this up as a regular thing," he announced as they were halfway through *Lethal Weapon 2*. "Twice a week I will pay you to come here and watch films and talk. Agreed?"

He wished he could see Gabriel's expression, guessed it would be a combination of shocked and resigned.

"Six will organize it with your…friend."

"Stefan could say no." Although Gabriel sounded intrigued at the thought of Cam booking him and what Stefan's reaction would be.

"He can try," Cam said darkly. "Also, I want you to think about leaving the place you share with Stefan and moving to Legacy Ranch. I will sponsor you financially to get you into college and into a job."

There was a movement, and Cam felt Gabriel stand up. "Night," he said.

"We're not done," Cam called after him, but he knew it was useless—the door slamming was indication enough that Gabriel hadn't liked what he'd said.

That night, Cam was restless, taking Gidget and

touring the hotel like he sometimes did when everyone was asleep. He got a sense of the hotel just after midnight, and there was peace there. He ended up in reception, taking a seat there, right in the back, Gidget curled up next to him. He chatted for a while with Doug the security guard, and Lacey, who manned the desk on tonight's shift between midnight and four. They talked weather, and films, and TV, and dogs, and everything that was normal.

He didn't sleep, though. He couldn't. He wasn't tired, and the thought of sleeping, until he'd found out what the answer was from this Stefan guy, was foreign to him.

The next booking was much the same, although Gabriel didn't try anything like sex. Cam gave him a drink, and Gabriel thanked him, but other than that there wasn't much in the way of talking. When Gabriel left Cam went back to prowling the corridors of the Royal with Gidget, stopping, chatting about everything and nothing, and not sleeping at all. He wanted to ask what kind of work Gabriel was getting. Six had said he hadn't been seen in the hotel, and Cam didn't know whether to worry or think that maybe Gabriel wasn't looking for work.

And why would he not look for work? Stupid.

Their third night together was different. Gabriel was edgy and restless. Cam didn't need to have sight to know something was wrong, and he didn't know how else to find out except to ask outright. Which he did.

But the answer surprised him.

"I've been thinking about things," Gabriel admitted. "That's all."

"You want to talk?"

"No."

"Okay then, choose a film."

They settled down to *Raiders of the Lost Ark*, and the silence between them was odd. Or was Cam making it odd? He wanted to ask what Gabriel had been thinking about. Was it about stopping coming here? Or something way more practical?

Halfway through the film, Gabriel turned it off, and after some moving on the sofa he sighed noisily.

"I really want to see your face," he said softly.

From the direction of the voice Cam could tell that Gabriel was facing him and talking right at him. So that statement was nothing but plain weird.

"You can see it," Cam said, and touched a finger to his lips. "It's right here."

"I want to see your face when you come." This time Gabriel was blunt. Then he tripped over the rest. "It's beautiful. You close your eyes, and you come, and it's the most beautiful thing I've ever seen."

"Gabriel…"

"And I don't get that with any of the others, I don't feel it, I don't want to see it. It's a job, it's nothing but a fucking job."

"I'm not paying you for sex, Gabriel."

"Then I'll suck you off for free." Gabriel placed a hand over his crotch and squeezed his cock, which had been hard from the moment Gabriel had made his announcement.

"No," Cam said, and pushed his hand away. "I can't think straight when you're touching me."

Gabriel made a small sound of disappointment, then made a move that Cam hadn't been expecting. The weight of Gabriel landed on him, straddling his lap, and when

Gabriel began to move, grinding against him, Cam's grip to ease him away turned into a grip to hold him close.

"Can I kiss you?" Gabriel asked, and placed his hands on Cam's shoulders. "I want to close my eyes and kiss you, and not get up until you've come over my hand or spilled in my mouth."

"Shit… Gabe…"

"And I want you to call me Gabe, I want you to tell me what to do, to make me suck you just by telling me, and I want it all to be free. I don't want you to pay me, I want you to pretend you want me for real, however difficult that is." He kissed Cam again, deeply, before Cam could even reassure him that he did want Gabriel for real.

The kiss turned to more, Gabriel encouraging Cam to lie flat on the sofa, placing his hands above his head and telling him not to move. He kissed every inch of skin he revealed, and teased Cam until he could do nothing except mewl his appreciation.

"I wish I could feel this," Gabriel murmured, so low Cam could have missed it if his hearing hadn't become so acute over the years. He wanted to know more, but then Gabriel got deadly focused, and in a short time Cam was coming, and Gabriel kissed him again and again, telling him how beautiful he was.

He left pretty soon after that, and neither of them said a thing.

When Gabriel had left, Cam went on his hotel walk, stopped and talked, but this time it wasn't because he couldn't sleep; it was because he didn't want to sleep in case he forgot a single moment of it all.

CHAPTER 13

Sleep just wasn't happening tonight, and Gabriel knew exactly why.

Cam's insistence on watching films, and eating Lay's chips, and talking about normal stuff, and then not having sex had forced Gabriel to snap tonight. He'd wanted Cam so badly that he hadn't been able to sit still on that damn sofa, and then the taste of Cam, the weight of him on Gabriel's tongue before watching him come, had been enough to have him getting hard.

Properly hard. Completely needy.

And then he'd arrived home and there had been no sign of Stefan but for a note on the fridge with details of Gabriel's next two bookings and a short sentence about how Stefan would be back in the morning.

Now Gabriel lay back in his bed, his hand on his cock and the image of Cam burned into his brain.

I wish I could feel this.

He couldn't believe he'd admitted that to Cam, like Cam would even be interested.

Sex for him was a duty, nothing more than a transaction, a way of getting what he wanted. He'd become a man in a way no person should have to, he knew that, but now at least when he had sex he received something in the bargain.

Not like back then. When his mom had died, she'd left him alone, but the ranch had taken him in. Hank Castille had taken him in.

It's okay, he'd said to the confused, heartbroken ten-year-old, *there will always be a place here*. He'd even dealt with the people the state had sent, or at least that was what he'd told Gabriel.

In hindsight, he wasn't sure that anyone outside the Bar Five had actually known who he was.

Frustrated with the direction his thoughts were taking him, back to a time he was happy to forget, he focused back on getting himself off.

Nothing was working—not gentle motion, not the pain of pinching, and not even when he pressed his other hand to his throat.

Stefan was right. He was utterly broken.

Softening and miserable, he buried himself under the covers and closed his eyes.

When he slept, he dreamed of pain, and the scent of horses, and the abject fear and horror that refused to leave him, and he woke up drenched with sweat. Stefan's door was shut as he walked past it to the shower, his wallet on the table by the door.

Stefan could give him the pain he needed to get off, and for a second the need to come outweighed the fact that going into Stefan's room would make him angry. Then it wouldn't be getting off, it would be a world of hurt that Gabriel didn't think he could handle tonight.

He skipped the shower, dressed, and took himself and his cell phone out of the apartment and down to the lobby, and for a second he stood looking out of the door, contemplating what to do. He felt the itch of wanting to talk to someone, to argue, to shout, and all he could think was which person would even want to talk to him?

He moved outside into the cool night air and parked himself on a bench outside the building. This wasn't the most expensive part of Dallas by any means, but it was a clean neighborhood, and quiet after dark, and this bench was out of everyone's view and no one could hear what he had to say.

He was lucky Stefan let him have a cell. It was only to be used in emergencies and for checking in with Stefan, and Gabriel wasn't allowed to store numbers in it, but still, it was a path to the world he tried to ignore.

A connection that he needed tonight.

He found the number easily enough and keyed the numbers into the pad, his thumb hovering over "OK". As he waited for the ring tone, he almost chickened out and ended the call, but the sleepy voice that answered was enough to shock him back to the here and now.

"Legacy Ranch, hello?" the voice said. Gabriel said nothing, his mouth dry. "Hi, this is Kyle, can I help you? Are you okay?"

Gabriel took the phone from his ear and stared at it. Did Kyle know it was him? Or did he have that question in a list for any lost soul who called the ranch? He ended the call.

And he stared at the sidewalk in front of the bench, his phone in his hand. The screen lit up with an incoming call. He stopped it immediately.

The screen lit again a few moments later. This time he stopped the call and pocketed his cell. He didn't want to talk to Kyle—it was ridiculous to even think of wanting to connect with the man.

He took his cell out again and looked at the three missed calls; clearly Kyle had tried again when the phone was in his pocket. He evidently wasn't giving up.

The next time it lit up, Gabriel slid the call to answer.

"Legacy is a safe place," Kyle said before Gabriel could say a word. "Whatever is happening with you, we can help."

Another set of standard words, no doubt. There were no safe places. What was he going to say to Kyle? After all, Kyle was doing okay with his boyfriend and his horses and *life*.

"They broke my legs," he blurted out. "They caught me running away and they got a baseball bat and they beat me so hard that they broke my legs and shattered my kneecaps. Did you know that?"

Of course Kyle didn't know that. How could he? He'd been long gone.

"Gabriel? Where are you?"

"And then, when they'd done that and they knew I couldn't run, they even took me to a hospital, said I'd had a fall. I still hurt when I kneel, and sometimes I limp, because after that first visit for medical help they never took me back. You know what I think now? If only at the hospital I'd told someone that I hadn't been in an accident, that Hank and Yuri had deliberately targeted me, then maybe someone would have given me my own kind of Legacy Ranch."

"It's not too late, Gabriel. Tell me where you are and I will find you and bring you here."

Gabriel felt a momentary bloom of hope, then it vanished. Stefan would be so mad, and what would happen if he had to come to Legacy to pick him up? Gabriel would be letting down so many clients.

"I can't leave Stefan." Even as he said it, he knew he wasn't being rational. He'd only spent a few nights on the streets when he got to Dallas, not even sixteen. He'd been lost and alone until Stefan had saved him. And now he'd lost count of the number of years he'd had with Stefan looking after him. Unbidden, his free hand went to his throat. Stefan knew what he needed. Stefan was a mix of father, and brother, and boss.

"You can," Kyle said softly, encouragingly. "And we can help you."

"No you can't. I don't want help."

"We can deal with Stefan—"

Gabriel ended the call.

Walking back into the apartment, he knew Stefan was awake. The place was flooded with light, and there was a tension in the air.

"Where were you, Angel?" Stefan asked from inside Gabriel's room, stepping out from it and into the light. "I woke up and your door was open."

"I couldn't sleep and I went for a walk." He smiled broadly at Stefan. Sometimes a ready smile worked on Stefan's temper, and it was worth a try, because he looked pissed.

"Let me see your phone," Stefan said, deceptively calm, holding out his hand.

Gabriel handed the phone over. There was no point in keeping it from Stefan; he'd end up getting it anyway.

"Who did you call? Was it Cameron Stafford? Because I'd hate for him to get the wrong idea. Hate to have to show him that he needs to remember you're a whore and not a person."

Gabriel felt a flash of defensiveness, then he remembered Six was always around Cam; nothing Stefan felt he had to do would hurt him. "No," he said.

"Then who was it?" Stefan asked, and pressed a few

buttons, to do what Gabriel didn't know. Then he held the cell out in front of him and put it on speaker phone, and at that moment Gabriel knew he was screwed.

Fear knifed at him, but he pulled his shoulders back and waited. The door to the apartment was right behind him; he could just turn and leave.

The call connected.

"Gabriel, we can help you."

Stefan ended the call and gently placed the cell on the table. "Who is that, Gabriel?"

"Legacy," Gabriel said, because Stefan would find out; what was the point in lying?

"Why are you calling them, Angel?" he asked, deceptively calm.

"Kyle was one of the boys from when I was at the Bar Five."

Stefan nodded. "Another lost and broken boy."

Gabriel recalled Kyle with the horses, Kyle with Jason, Kyle not in fear of his fucking life every single waking second.

"Yes," he said instead.

"Go to bed, Angel," Stefan murmured, his arms crossed over his chest.

That was it? Stefan wasn't going to tell him he was wrong, or shout at him? Gratitude and warmth spread through Gabriel, and he smiled at Stefan. "Okay." He went to walk past Stefan, dodging slightly to the right when the impulse to hug him struck him. Stefan hated the shows of affection that Gabriel wanted to give at the best of times, and it was two a.m., but his guard down, Gabriel felt light, wanted, needed. Stefan reached out and gripped his arm, just a little too tightly. Gabriel didn't pull away.

"You're nothing without me, right? I'm the one you come to if you need to talk," he said calmly.

Gabriel looked at Stefan and nodded. "I know."

"Seemingly not enough," Stefan said, and he smiled sadly. "You know what I have to do."

Gabriel nodded. He knew he'd fucked up. "Please don't hurt me," he said. He always said that.

Stefan shook his head. "I don't want to, Angel. But someone has to look out for you."

"Please—"

Stefan pinned him to the bed, his hands around Gabriel's throat, but he wasn't angry, his expression was utterly focused. "If I killed you, no one would care, you know that right?"

Gabriel whimpered. All he could think was that Cam would care.

Wouldn't he?

"I could press harder and harder until every breath was gone from you, and you'd let me, wouldn't you?"

No. Don't hurt me. I want to live.

But the pressure on his throat was too much, and his vision was darkening, and he could only think of one thing.

Stefan was right. No one wanted Gabriel Reyes.

CHAPTER 14

Julie sat in front of Cam, knotting her hands nervously. "I didn't know what to say," she began.

"Start from the beginning," Six said from behind him. "Tell Mr. Stafford what you told me."

"He's always quick to get angry when he's here—Mitchell, I mean—and I know we shouldn't speak out about him, being that he's family and married to your sister, but he scares some of the young girls."

"How?" Cam asked, his stomach in knots. He was sick of feeling this way, like his life was out of control and the people around him were being hurt.

"I wouldn't say anything, but I'm on maternity leave after this Friday and I can give my notice here and now if you don't want me back."

There was defiance in her tone, and Cam was proud of her.

"Start from the beginning."

By the time she left, she'd stopped crying, and Cam had said he would deal with it. He was seething and worried, and pissed that he'd missed so much.

"Get Mitchell up here," he said.

Mitchell was in the hotel on a fact-finding task set by Sebastian—something about market share, not that Cam had agreed to any of it.

As soon as Six had left, Cam called Sophie, but yet again it went to voicemail. This time he left a long, detailed message. "Sophie, it's Cam. I'm your brother and I love you, and I will always be here for you. Call me."

Mitchell arrived five minutes later, his breath a little on the wheezy side, which made Cam think that Six had somehow coerced the man to come to the office.

"Six, can you wait outside?" Cam asked, and Six left, shutting the door behind him. Cam stood up and rounded the desk, leaning back on it with a sense of where Mitchell was standing.

"What's wrong?" Mitchell asked. "Your ape was most insistent; he needs to know who I am and back off."

"I had to make him go outside," Cam began calmly. "Because Six wants to kill you." He heard the gasp but didn't give Mitchell time to talk. "You will treat my sister with respect. You are not a Stafford, you are a wannabe who will be out the door once I explain to Dad how you have insulted several of my staff and how forcing them into the locker room and pawing them counts as sexual harassment."

"What the hell—"

"Shut. Up. I have several of my staff willing to put your advances in writing. Some already have. I will be filing them here, and you will not step foot inside my hotel again."

"You can't do this—"

"You see, Mitchell, actually I can." He raised his voice. "Six, you can come back in." The door opened. "If you could escort this man from the premises."

"I can take myself out," Mitchell snapped, and left. "You'll be hearing from my lawyers."

The door slammed after him.

"Six, go to Sophie. Help her; tell her to come here. Don't let Mitchell take it out on her."

"On it."

When Six arrived back a little after eight that evening with a tearful Sophie, Cam wondered for a moment if he'd completely fucked up. She might hate him. She might tell him he was wrong.

But all she did was hug him, and they sat on the sofa quietly for the longest time with *Armageddon* running in the background. When it ended and she'd cried so much it broke Cam's heart, she simply held him close.

"I'll take one of the rooms here," she said, "if that's okay."

"Six will put you in a suite."

"There's no need—"

"You're my sister and I love you. This is a family hotel."

"Love you too, big brother."

Cam rolled over in bed, the shrill alarm of his phone waking him from fragmented dreams in which he was being chased by Mitchell with a cleaver, not that he really knew what Mitchell looked like, but he picture a giant ogre and went with that in his dreams.

He scrambled for his cell, disoriented, and connected the call.

"What's wrong?" he answered.

"You can have him," a voice said. "You fucked with his head and he's no good to me. Two million and you can have him."

"Who is this?"

A laugh echoed down the line. "You know who it is. You have an hour." The phone went dead, and all Cam did was reach over and press the emergency button. In less than a minute, Six was in the room and Cam was half dressed.

"What?" Six snapped. "Is it Mitchell? I should have dealt with him more than leaving him at the bus station without his wallet."

"No, it's not him. We need to get money; we need to save Gabriel." He pulled on the shirt he'd discarded before bed, fumbling with the buttons, losing all control of how he usually managed to get dressed.

"Save Gabriel. What?" Hands gripped Cam's arms, stopping him from moving. "Talk to me."

"That man you book with, Stefan, he called me. He wants money for Gabriel."

Six shook him a little, and he cursed.

"We're not paying someone for Gabriel," Six said, his tone calm, his hold still firm.

But it wasn't the tone that made Cam snap—it was the desperate need to do something, anything, and knowing that Six had to help him.

"Fuck's sake, Six, we have to go—"

"Okay, calm the hell down." Six released his grip, and Cam wobbled a little before pulling himself together and reaching for where he knew he'd put his jacket. Six beat him to it, helping to put it on.

Cam whistled for Gidget and petted her, "Stay here," he said, talking like she would even understand that Six was with him and he was going to be okay. She nosed his hand and whined soft and low, but then Cam heard her turning circles on her bed. He couldn't think about Gidget. He couldn't even get his head around what they needed to do. Only in the car did he remember the money again.

"How much money can I get now?"

"It's five a.m.," Six snapped.

"We can transfer it—"

"Cam, enough. Let me think, okay?"

Cam subsided, feeling like everything was out of control, then abruptly knowing that Six would be the one to take the brunt of whatever was happening here.

"Thank you," Cam murmured, scrubbing at his eyes with his fists. "I never say it, but thank you."

"You won't be thanking me if I kill the bastard."

"You're not hurting Gabriel. This isn't his fault—"

"Jesus, Cam, I'm not hurting Gabriel."

They drove in silence again, but the way that Six took corners felt like they were traveling at speed. What if they picked up a cop? Did they want the cops involved in this?

The car came to a sharp stop and Six opened his door. "Stay here."

Cam wasn't doing that. "He called me," he said, and opened his own door, wincing as it hit something that sounded metal, probably a fire hydrant.

Six laid a hand on Cam's arm. "But he's dealing with me."

There was danger in Six's tone, and Cam knew he had to be realistic. Whatever was happening with Gabriel and this Stefan guy wouldn't be helped by him getting in the way.

"I have the money," he said, a little desperately.

"Cam, I know. Leave this to me."

"He may not want to leave," Cam murmured. "He thinks Stefan is his only choice."

Six rested a hand on his knee, squeezed it. "Stay here and lock the doors after me."

Cam nodded. He could do that. It was pretty much all he could do, but it was something, right?

Six left, Cam locked the car, and then all he could do was wait.

* * * * *

Gabriel shifted in the chair that Stefan had recommended he sit on. His tone had been more forceful than suggesting, but Gabriel wasn't arguing. He hadn't laid a hand on him, nor shown him why he'd been wrong—all he'd done was make a single phone call in his room, and then he'd come back out and sat on the sofa, staring right at Gabriel.

And all Gabriel could do was wait for the ax to fall. This was worse than Stefan punishing him and reassuring him of his place in the world. This was different. Wrong.

"You remember I took you in," Stefan said calmly, collected and focused.

What was Gabriel supposed to say? That question had been asked so many times, and it seemed he never answered the right way. If he said a simple yes, then he wasn't thankful enough. If he said yes and thanked Stefan, then that was too submissive and pathetic.

"I do," he finally said, and waited for the explosion that always occurred after this trick question.

Stefan nodded. "It wasn't enough money," he said. "That pitiful amount you paid me wasn't enough to pay for everything I've given you. A place to sleep. A career. You get that, right?"

Everything always came back to money. The PI who'd tracked him down had given him a check with the name Darren Castille on the bottom and a letter, and Stefan had taken the check and the letter. He'd never seen either again. But he knew Stefan had cashed that check somehow, because he'd told him over and over again that it hadn't been enough.

Nothing Gabriel did was ever enough.

Why don't you stand up to Stefan? The peace in this room, this fragile peace that could snap into violence at any moment, was a space for him to think, to pray that maybe this time the violence would be enough to end everything for him.

He wanted to say goodbye to Cam, though, and maybe watch one more film with him and eat all his chips. Because Cam meant something to a broken man. Not that Gabriel deserved it.

"I'm sorry," he murmured, because that was what Stefan expected whenever money came up.

"You should sign over your savings to me. That will make us even."

Gabriel's insides knotted. The money he'd saved was to pay back Darren Castille the blood money he'd been given. And he was so close to having it all. "No," he said, and tried to make himself smaller in the chair.

Stefan half rose to his feet, temper in every line of him, then he subsided back onto the sofa, and he was smiling.

"I'll take it anyway," he said. "What are you going to do to stop me?" He laughed at his own statement, like it was some huge joke.

"That isn't even my money," Gabriel said, aware he was pushing this too hard. Why was Stefan just sitting there? Why didn't he beat Gabriel, or hurt him in some other way? He could handle the pain, but he didn't know how to handle this weird face-off. Was this just another way to mess with him? Something new that Gabriel hadn't had time to build a mental wall against?

"Doesn't matter," Stefan said, and examined his nails. "I have the bank of Cameron Stafford ready to bankroll you."

Cam's name made his spiraling thoughts come to a grinding halt.

"What?"

Stefan casually looked at his watch. "He'll be here soon. Two million for your sorry ass, and there will be more where that came from."

"Leave Cam alone," Gabriel said softly, a low warning that made him feel sick to the stomach. Stefan couldn't touch Cam.

"I'm not touching Cam," Stefan said with a grin. "I just need to hurt you."

"That won't work, he doesn't care about me."

"You're wrong, Angel, he thinks something of you," Stefan said. "He's a rich man who can pay for your used ass for a very long time."

"No," Gabriel said, and he pushed himself shakily to his feet. "Leave. Him. Alone."

Stefan stood as well, and a grin split his face. "What are you going to do to stop me?"

Gabriel clenched his fists and took an unsteady step forward. "No," he said.

"What will you do? Hit me?" Stefan laughed. He was a big man, strong, and Gabriel was nothing against him, but he was close to losing it.

The thought of Stefan hurting Cam, taking money from him, was wrong.

It was all fucking wrong.

There was a knock on the door, and Stefan's grin expanded even more. "Showtime," he said.

He crossed to the door, but as soon as he'd opened it, the door flew in forcefully, knocking him to the floor.

Six stood there, cold focus in his eyes, and he glanced briefly at Gabriel. Then he picked up a floored Stefan and pinned him by his neck to the wall, his feet dangling. Stefan was scrambling to pull Six off, but he'd finally met someone bigger and stronger than him.

"You have belongings here?" Six asked, and Gabriel realized he was talking to him. "Snap out of it, Gabriel. You have stuff you need to collect?"

"Yes, I…"

"Get them."

Stefan made a choking sound, but Six didn't move, even when Stefan's foot connected with his knee. He just moved to pin him bodily.

"Gabriel, get your fucking stuff."

Gabriel did as he was told, going to his room, looking wildly at what he had. Nothing.

He had nothing. No photos, no books, no clothes that he wanted. Nothing.

He came back out. Stefan was quieter, still pinned, his eyes closed.

"Cam is downstairs. Get to the car and wait for me."

Gabriel sidled past Stefan, who opened his eyes and stared right at him. "I'll kill you," he spluttered, but Six pushed him harder, and this time his eyes rolled back in his head.

"Get. To. The. Car."

"Are you killing him?" Gabriel asked, and he couldn't believe those words had left his mouth. What was he asking? It was like another man was inside his head.

"Do time for a piece of shit like him? We'll see. Now go."

Gabriel scrambled out of the room, down the stairs, and burst out onto the early morning street, coming face to face with Cam leaning on the hood of a large SUV that had been parked haphazardly up on the sidewalk.

"Cam," Gabriel murmured. The shock of what he was seeing, of what had just happened, was too much. He stepped back and turned on his heel. He didn't know where he was going to go, but Six would look out for Cam.

"Gabriel? Wait."

He turned back and saw that Cam had moved away from the car, his hand out in front of him like he expected to feel Gabriel there.

"I have to go."

"What happened?" Cam asked, and took a step toward him, knocking into the fire hydrant on the corner. He stumbled a little, but righted himself immediately. "Are you okay?"

"Six is talking to Stefan." He didn't know how else to explain what was happening inside that apartment. Was Six going to kill Stefan? Would Gabriel's life end with that of the man who'd shaped him? Tears came unbidden to him, rolling down his cheeks, and he couldn't believe he was standing there in the middle of the fucking street bawling like a baby.

Cam moved closer, and Gabriel was frozen in place.

"Come here," Cam said—not an order, just a plea.

Gabriel took a step closer to Cam, then stopped. "I have to go," he said.

"Okay," Cam said, and nodded. "I'll take you wherever you need to go."

Where was he going to go? He had his savings, but he wanted them to repay the awful debt that Stefan had made him take on. He didn't want blood money from his time at the Bar Five. He wanted nothing from his childhood.

Except his mom.

"I really want my mom," he said.

"We can take you anywhere," Cam said immediately.

"Mom's gone. She died when I was a kid. You can't give me my mom."

"How can I help you? I can take you to the hotel?"

"No."

"Legacy, then."

Legacy would take him in for a while so he could get his bearings, and he knew that the place was close to the ranch where Darren worked. He could take out all his money, pay Darren, maybe get some sleep before he fell to the ground and slept right here.

"Legacy," he agreed.

The door to the building slammed open and Six came out. He wasn't covered in blood, he didn't seem in a hurry, and he didn't say a thing about what had happened.

"We're taking Gabriel to Legacy Ranch," Cam said. Seemed like he wasn't questioning Six about what had happened either. Like maybe he didn't care what Six had done to Stefan.

"Is he dead?" Gabriel asked. Half of Gabriel wanted Stefan dead so he'd be free. The other half was ashamed of feeling that way. Stefan had saved him from the streets.

He saved me.

And now Six and Cam have saved me.

Why can't I save myself?

"No, I didn't kill him. Get in the damn car."

The journey to Legacy Ranch took enough time for Gabriel to think about everything that had happened. The pain and the fear and the self-loathing. By the time they reached the place he hoped he could call home for at least a couple of days, it was eight a.m. and the light was too bright on his tired eyes. Six pulled up at the end of the road and stayed in the car. Only Cam and Gabriel got out, and the door to the ranch house opened, Kyle standing in the doorway with Jason at his side.

"You know where I am," Cam said, and held out his right hand. "When you're ready, you know how to reach me."

"Why would you want that?" He couldn't help asking the question. Why would this strong man want someone who was as broken and twisted as Gabriel?

In answer, Cam moved into his space, sliding his hands up Gabriel's arms and finally cradling his face. Gabriel was frozen in place. He couldn't even breathe. His chest felt tight. And then Cam did the unthinkable. He pressed a soft kiss to Gabriel's lips, then slanted his mouth to deepen the kiss. Taken by surprise, Gabriel reciprocated. He'd never tasted anything like this, never felt the connection in a simple kiss.

And then Cam stepped back. "I'll visit. You don't need to see me, but I want to know you're okay."

"I'm not staying here that long."

Cam kissed him again, right on the tip of his nose and then each eye before resting his lips on Gabriel's again, then he moved away.

"You know where I am," he said.

Gabriel watched him get into the car, and then as Six backed up the drive, until all that was left of them was a trail of dust. He rubbed at his chest. He wanted Cam to come back, wanted selfishly to have another kiss, to depend on Cam to fix this, to have Six next to him all the time to stop anyone hurting him.

But he wasn't worth that kind of love.

So he walked to Kyle, who extended a hand, which Gabriel shook.

"We have your room ready," Kyle said.

And completely mortified, Gabriel followed him in.

CHAPTER 15

Kyle was quiet. He had this way about him that was serious and thoughtful, and he was the direct opposite of Jason, who seemed to bounce from one thing to another. But they balanced each other and they seemed genuinely happy.

Jason was Kyle's right-hand man, and it was Kyle who ran Legacy Ranch and handed out chores. Like today it was Gabriel's turn to muck out and brush down the horses, all four of them. Including his horse.

Yep. His horse.

Day three, and a man he half recognized from his last abortive visit to Legacy had arrived atop a horse, another on a rein behind him.

"This is Pixie," the man had said as he'd dismounted. He'd extended a hand. "Jack," he'd introduced himself. Gabriel had wiped his hands on his pants and shaken Jack's firmly. "Now, don't be fooled by the cutesy name, you can blame my youngest daughter for that; everything is called Pixie at the moment."

"Okay," Gabriel murmured, because Jack appeared to expect a response, and that was pretty much all Gabriel had. The horse had been big, a dark brown, with huge melty eyes and a twitchy nose. Then it had hit him. Jack wanted him to take the reins and put Pixie in one of the empty stables.

He could do that. It was his third day, and he'd moved up from hating the sight of the horses and the barns to actually stepping foot inside. He hadn't lasted long in there—the scent of hay and horses, the noises, and all he could recall was pain.

"She's all yours while you're here," Jack had continued.

"I don't want a horse."

"Every person who stays here helps out with the charitable side of the ranch, looking out for rescued animals."

Oh. Now he got it. The broken human got paired with a damaged horse and magic happened. Gabriel had thought at that moment that the chance of a horse doing anything for him was remote.

Day five, though, and he'd managed to stable Pixie on his own, and even allowed her to nudge at him without flinching.

And now Kyle was standing there looking in on him, and he was quiet and deadly serious.

"Clair is here," he said as he moved the wheelbarrow a little to help as Gabriel worked at the back of the stall.

For a brief moment, Gabriel didn't know who Kyle meant. And then he did. He moved another pile of manure from floor to barrow, then stopped and leaned on the shovel.

"I'm supposed to talk to her." *Like I'm supposed to bond with my horse.*

"No," Kyle said with a smile, and leaned over the stall wall to fuss at Pixie. He ran his hands over the scars on her flanks; marks put there by owners who'd abused the poor animal. Pixie carried scars that were visible, but under it all she hadn't lost the ability to trust.

She relied on Gabriel. Trusted him. Showed affection.

How could an animal forgive being shown nothing but

pain? He couldn't forget it, let alone forgive.

"No I don't have to see her?"

"Not at all. That isn't what Legacy does. This isn't forced counseling—this place is all about peace." He glanced out at the land beyond the barn door and gestured toward it. "A man can get lost in all this space."

"I used to love the horses," Gabriel said. Then realized he'd said something that might invite a discussion and he set about shoveling more manure.

"She's here all day. Jason is giving her riding lessons, which are going well. So if you want to talk, I think she has a ride planned this afternoon, or maybe you can grab her and have a quick chat if you need her."

"Thank you," Gabriel said, because that was the polite thing to say.

"Right. I'm fixing the bathroom in pod eight, so you know where to find me."

He tipped his hat and left. Pod eight was right next to Gabriel's seven, and was an empty room. Some girl called Marianna had been and gone the week before he'd arrived. She'd run here, and then run away. He knew, because Jason had told him that Kyle had taken it super personally that she'd left, like he should have known. Before she left, she'd trashed the room—written all over the walls, apparently, and taken an ax to everything inside.

How fucked up was it that Gabriel could understand that kind of anger?

He was consumed by anger and his own self-loathing, and the idea of taking an ax and destroying everything in this room made him itch with need.

His cell vibrated, and like he'd been trained to expect it, he smiled. Cameron had taken to texting him at weird times of the day, stupid little anecdotes about what he was doing, about the hotel, Gidget, and about how Six asked about him.

Probably to make sure he wasn't coming back, was all Gabriel had thought when he'd heard that last bit of news. He pulled the cell out of his pocket. Reading the text would be a welcome distraction from having to think about Clair and her up-in-the-air counseling.

"Six is grumpy as fuck," the text began. "Send help." After that was a selection of emojis, including one of a smiling poop. *Not sure what that's supposed to mean.*

He texted back a smile. That was mostly what he sent. There were never questions in the random texts. Never a "how are you" or questions about Stefan. Nope, everything was chatty. Happy. The first time he'd got a text, he'd freaked out and it had taken him an hour to open it, and then he'd had to make sure he was entirely alone in case Cam was texting to tell him Stefan had caused problems.

A small part of Gabriel wanted to know what Stefan was doing. Had Six scared him off? Threatened him? Buried him in some remote Texas field?

But mostly he wanted to know for sure that Cam was safe.

Another text came in. "I want to take you to dinner," it said.

"What?" Gabriel said out loud, Pixie looking at him and huffing at his shoulder. Idly, he patted her coat and re-read the text. Those seven words made him feel weird. Really weird.

And he had nothing to say.

So he finished his chores, ignored his cell, and went

inside for lunch. Only Clair was in there, sitting at the big table with papers spread out in front of her. She looked hot and red in the face, her long, dark hair pulled back from her face in a messy ponytail.

She looked up at the door and smiled. "Hello, Gabriel."

"Hi," he said. "I'm making lunch."

Everyone was responsible for their own lunch here, and that was part of the day Gabriel enjoyed. His appetite was still for shit, but he liked rummaging in the fully stocked fridge for ingredients to make up sandwiches.

"There's coffee there I made earlier."

He nodded and opened the fridge, pulling out salad and ham, then found the bread, and all that time Clair was reading through papers and tutting and sighing. He almost asked her what was wrong, but he didn't. Instead he thought about it being lunchtime, about making his lunch, and about her maybe not having eaten.

And that was the thought process that led to his first session with Clair. He offered her lunch, and before he knew it the clock showed four p.m. and they'd filled the entire time talking.

"No two relationships are the same," she summarized as they sipped fresh coffee.

"So why do I feel like I miss Stefan?"

"Because you still feel like he saved you from a fate that was so much worse. He was better than the options you had, and maybe when he first took you from that corner, he had your best interests at heart."

Even knowing that wasn't true didn't push away the insistent nag of need he had to see Stefan again.

"What's unhealthy in one relationship may be abusive

in another. Maybe he never went far enough for your brain to register abuse."

"He checked my cell phones. Hell, it wasn't even my cell phone. He was always angry and jealous, never had a kind word to say, and his temper scared me." He counted off the things that Clair had helped him identify in the toxic link he'd had with Stefan. "He hurt me, so badly at times that I couldn't work, and then he'd be angry that I couldn't work. I had a friend once—he was a porter at a hotel we had this standing booking at. I wasn't allowed to talk to him. He was possessive and erratic."

"Today is a start," Clair said. "You now need to let it settle. I'm back tomorrow if you want to talk."

"You know what scares me the most?"

Clair shook her head slightly and waited for him to expand.

"I'm terrified I left to make myself a better person for him. Because I felt like I'd disappointed him."

"I understand that. You mean it wasn't because you'd come to any realization that you were better off away from him."

"I could have run off so many times and I didn't."

She reached over and clasped his hand. "It's okay."

Gabriel wished it felt okay.

Marianna, the girl who had trashed her place with an ax, arrived back at Legacy some days later without fanfare, appearing in the kitchen, her face a mess of crying, her eyes ringed with darkness. Kyle was on his feet before she could even speak, and he pulled her in for a hug. She was sobbing so hard that Gabriel didn't know where to look. So he took out his cellphone and re-read messages that Cam had sent him. They made him feel better, and when Kyle and Marianna moved from the doorway, he slipped out.

She only lasted another day, wouldn't stop crying, and he knew how she was feeling. Like her whole world was gone, destroyed. Kyle didn't spot her leaving—neither did Jason.

He did.

God knew what made him do it, but he followed her, caught up with her about a hundred feet from Legacy, and moved to block her way.

"Hey," he said, because it seemed like the right place to start.

"Get out of my way," she said, her expression dead, her eyes sad. She took a step to move around him, but he blocked her, and she shoved at his chest.

"You can't leave," he said. Even though he'd wanted to leave a hundred times, he owed it to himself to stay, to make himself better for Cam's faith in him. He didn't want to stay—hell, half of him wanted to take Marianna by the hand and walk off this damn land.

But where would that leave him? Where would he go? What would he do?

Abruptly, he knew he had to make Marianna stay.

How do I do that?

"Who hurt you?" he asked gently, aware he could spook her with one wrong word. Green eyes widened, and she stepped back like he'd hit her. Then the shock vanished and instead the mask of control slipped down.

"My cousin raped me. I was ten. He hurt me, and no one believed me, and he did it again and again."

She was trying to make him feel something. Disgust,

maybe. But he had stories.

Gabriel didn't have to think what to say. "When my mom died, the guy she worked for, he would lock me away and bring me out for parties where I was forced to suck men off, and they would rape me and hurt me and I couldn't get away."

"I tried to get away. My dad dragged me back."

"I tried to get away. They broke my legs."

"I cried every night."

"And all day."

Marianna looked at him, and her mask slipped, her green eyes filling with tears. "Why did he want to hurt me? What did I do?"

Fuck. Gabriel wished he had an answer, that he could stand there and tell her that everything was okay and there was a reason for the insanity that had hurt her. He had nothing. Instead he answered with a question of his own.

"Why did those men think it was okay to use a kid so badly?" he murmured.

She nodded. They understood each other's pain.

"I don't want to stay," she said, and thumbed back at the ranch. "They try to make me stay."

The words were heavy with meaning, and abruptly Gabriel felt something shift inside him.

"They said I could leave anytime I wanted," he said. "They didn't try to make me stay."

Marianna looked at her feet. "They say that," she mumbled. "They don't mean it."

Gabriel held out a hand, and she grasped it, hard, their fingers lacing.

"Let's go talk to them."

She tugged at his hold, but he didn't let go, and she

wasn't pulling hard. Maybe she needed someone strong enough to help her. Maybe he could be that person one day?

"Let's go find Kyle," he said.

"What if he tries to make me stay?"

"I won't let him."

They walked back to the ranch, their hands still clasped, and found Kyle with the horses. He gave them all his attention as soon as he saw them.

"Hey guys," he said, looking at them and then at the clasped hands. "Everything okay?"

Gabriel cleared his throat, and Marianna edged closer to him so their elbows knocked. She was looking for support, and he might not be the right person to give it, but he could at least try.

"I wanted to leave," Gabriel began, "so you got me a cab and you let me leave."

Kyle wiped his hands on his jeans and nodded. "We did." He sounded like he was looking for a reason why Gabe was talking about that.

"If Marianna wanted to leave, you'd call her a cab, right?"

Kyle frowned, and Gabriel tensed. Right here and now, Kyle's answer was vital.

"Yeah," he said. "I would want her to stay so she could feel like she had a safe place, a home, but if she wanted to leave, we would help where we could."

Next to him, Marianna relaxed a little—he could feel it in the way her grasp on his hand lessened. She wouldn't entirely believe Kyle, because she'd been hurt like he had, but this was a start.

Right there and then, Gabriel felt a tiny piece of his

heart shift. Was it possible that one day he could be a person that someone actually *needed* in their lives?

The text from Cam the next day was a picture of Gidget and the caption, *I ate a bar of soap*. Next to Gidget was a soap wrapper, one of those tiny hotel ones, and Gidget had the biggest doggie grin.

"Uh-oh," Gabe sent with a quirky smiley face.

"Then she was sick over my shoes," Cam texted. "I didn't see it, but I could smell it."

"Poor Gidget."

"Poor shoes." Cam added the usual emojis, including the poop one.

That was the end of the conversation apart from one final text. "Did you think about dinner?"

Gabriel ignored that. Yes, he had, but sitting opposite Cam after everything that had happened, with all those weird feeling of attraction inside him, was more than he could bear thinking about.

"So he keeps suggesting we meet for dinner," Gabriel tagged on at the end of the latest session. They'd been talking about how there was a difference between naïve and eternally optimistic. That had come about because they'd spent most of the hour talking about Cam.

"Will you?" Clair asked, and rested her chin on her fingers.

"What? See him?"

"Yeah."

"I don't know."

"You're still tied to Stefan in your head," Clair

observed, and Gabriel couldn't argue. He couldn't get Stefan out of his head; well, not entirely, anyway. The man was like a poison that made you feel the best you ever had before killing you. What was Stefan to him? Not a friend, that was for sure.

"I think you should meet Cam for dinner."

"I'm not ready." To leave Legacy, to face other people. He was safe here with Marianna and the horses, and these chats with Clair.

"Get him to come here. Make him lunch. That way you won't be away from Legacy and you could see what's there between you."

"What if there's nothing? What if that kiss meant nothing? What if me getting hard is nothing?"

There weren't many secrets between them now; after all, they'd been talking for three weeks on and off. He texted Cam right there and then, extended the invitation for him to come to lunch tomorrow or the next day. Or any day. Preferably a few months into the future.

He pressed send. "Tell me again what you said."

"What part?"

"The part about self-worth."

Clair hesitated momentarily. "You don't need to hear it again. You know it word for word.

"Then if I know it, why do I still feel like I'm worth nothing?"

She didn't answer, simply looked at him steadily, and he closed his eyes.

As long as I believe I deserved the abuse, I won't feel worthy to have a relationship

He wished he could get over his fucking head. Sex was the only currency he understood, and he didn't want to meet up with Cam and fall back on that.

Cam replied in less than ten minutes, suggesting the next day. And that was it. Done.

CHAPTER 16

When he got the text finally giving in to lunch, Cam had to replay it three times to make sure he'd heard it right.

Even now, in the car with Six at his side, he replayed the message and his reply.

Six had a very strong opinion on what he was doing today. "I still think this is stupid."

"So you said."

"Mitchell was sniffing around what you're doing, and you know your dad will use any excuse to put him in as co-manager. Going on a date with a hooker has to be right up there as a reason to push you aside."

"And like I said every other time you mentioned that, this is my hotel, free and clear. There's nothing Dad can do."

Six muttered something that Cam couldn't hear, and he didn't want to know what it was because he had lunch to concentrate on.

"He's standing waiting for you," Six informed him when the car stopped.

"What's he wearing?"

Six paused, and Cam could imagine him giving Cam a look of despair.

"Jeans, kinda faded, a plaid shirt, mostly blue, and he's got a Stetson on his head. Hell, the man's gone full-on cowboy."

Cam smoothed his own jeans—new, designer—and thought about the shirt he was wearing. It was blue, the same shade as his eyes, or at least he assumed so. The braille inside just said blue, which implied that it wasn't light blue or dark blue, because if it were either of those it would say so. At least he could tell the collar was flat, and Six wouldn't let him go out looking like a moron.

And yes, he was freaking out, just a little.

"I want it on record that this is a fucking insane idea," Six growled.

"Noted."

"I don't get it. Do you think he's gold under the tarnish, a hooker with a heart, like this is a Hollywood movie?"

Cam pulled at the material of his pants. What did he say?

"There's a connection, Six. Something real."

"You don't know what you're talking about."

"Why? Because I'm blind?" Cam snapped, and made to climb out of the car.

Six stopped him. "Really? After all these years, you're going there?"

The sentiment behind the words—sadness, a bleakness that hit Cam squarely in the chest—had him turning back in Six's direction. "No, I'm not, but after all these years, you know I have as much of a sixth sense as you do."

"But what about Adam?"

"He was a mistake. I should have listened to my gut, but I was desperate for something, a connection, and I never had that with Adam, which shows how much of one I think I have with Gabriel."

"You *think* you have. He's damaged goods, Cam."

That made Cam smile. He knew that. But hell... "I'm part of a dysfunctional family that equates blind with useless and gay with weak. I haven't had a hug from my parents since they sat in that doctor's room with me and heard there wasn't anything anyone could do to stop me going blind. I think I'm damaged goods as well. You're more my dad than my own father."

"Jesus, Cam," Six said with feeling. "You know I'm only... Jeez..."

"It's okay," Cam murmured, and opened the door, the heat of a Texas summer flooding into the car. "I never say the right things."

This time Six pulled him back, held him, and it was tight and close and Cam leaned into the hug.

"I'll be here," Six said.

Cam nodded into the hold. "You always are. Thank you."

With the car door shut behind him, he didn't know which way to face, but he didn't need to worry, because Gabriel was there, standing close to him, the scent of him subtly changed. Instead of cologne, it was work, and soap and normality, and it was sexy and endearing all at the same time.

"Gabe?" Cam asked. He wanted to pull Gabriel into his arms and kiss him so hard, but he wasn't sure Gabriel would want that. Was he even on the same page?

And then he was under no illusion on exactly what Gabriel was feeling.

Gabriel cradled his face and kissed him in the summer sun, and the kiss was deep and needy. Every single worry, every doubt, every word that people sent his way to get him to back off, they all vanished. He loved this man, wanted him. He wouldn't say it, but for him this could be forever.

Cam wound his arms around Gabriel's neck and held on tight. Six couldn't move the car while he was pressed against it, but none of that mattered.

"I missed you," Cam said between kisses.

"I have so much to tell you," Gabriel said back, but he didn't let go. He was hard against Cam's thigh.

I want you to come. I want to feel you...

Gabriel finally backed away and tugged him along, slowing when there was uneven ground, which he warned Cam about as they walked. The ground didn't become floor, and the heat of the sun was still there, so they weren't heading indoors, and then the scent of horses hit him.

"I want you to meet Pixie," Gabriel said, and guided Cam to a hard wooden fence. "Put out your hand."

Cam did as he was told, completely trusting that Gabriel wasn't setting him up for something stupid. Something pushed against his hand, soft—velvet-soft, actually—and he smiled.

"Tell me about her."

"She's a dark brown quarter horse, stands fifteen hands tall, and she has this white strip on her nose. She's my horse."

Gabriel said it so proudly that Cam's chest tightened. "You have a horse."

"Everyone at Legacy gets a horse—it's a therapy thing." Gabriel didn't sound resentful of the idea of therapy. If anything, he appeared laid-back and accepting.

"She's beautiful," Cam said, stroking the soft nose and laughing at the snort of breath on his neck as the horse nuzzled him. "If I'd known, I would have brought a carrot or something."

"Thank you," Gabriel said, leaning into him.

"For the carrot? I didn't actually bring one—"

"For what you and Six did. For coming to get me."

"Always," Cam said. They kissed again, but were broken apart by a huffing Pixie, who evidently thought kissing in a barn was a bad thing.

Cam couldn't agree with that.

"I'll show you my room, hold on." The terrain changed from rough and hard to smooth floor, and it was cool in here. "So there's a bed, a small bathroom, and every room has a desk you can put photos on and study at, that kind of thing."

"Are you going to be studying?" Cam said, and felt for the bed, sitting on the side of it.

"I don't know what I'm doing from one day to the next. I know I feel changed—not better, but different. I've been speaking to this woman called Clair who's helping me get my head around everything, and also to Jason. He's the boyfriend of the guy who runs this place, and he used to work the streets for money. We have a lot in common."

"What you did is a very real part of you," Cam said. He wanted Gabriel to hear that Cam wasn't going to forget what he'd done, had to do, been made to do. That was Gabriel's journey to here, and it wouldn't change.

"Clair is helping a lot." The bed dipped as Gabriel sat next to him. "And I have you as a friend."

"I'll always be your friend," Cam insisted. "But, it's more than just friendship for me." He wanted to talk about the connection between them, about the future and the past, and he wanted to tell Gabriel that he wasn't going anywhere. He said none of it, because the time wasn't right. It would be one day, just not today. Seemed like

Gabriel had other ideas.

"I don't get why you'd feel that way. You could have anyone. You have money, and a hotel, and the chance to hook up with a hundred eligible guys who your family would approve of."

They didn't get a chance to talk about it further. A knock on the door and a shouted "Food!" had Gabriel standing up. "C'mon—Kyle and Jason are doing food, and I want you to meet them. And Marianna—she's my friend, but you need to be careful with her, because she's kinda hurt."

"Okay."

"So eat all the food, talk to the people, and then we get some quiet time. Right?"

"I want time alone with you," Cam confirmed simply, and evidently that was all Gabriel needed to hear.

The afternoon went too fast. They ate barbecue, but there was a lot of time when it was just Gabriel and Cam. Six even joined them for food, but that didn't last long, and he made his excuses and sat inside with a book, with Clair who had arrived just after lunch. Cam wanted to talk to her, to get a feel for what he could do for the best.

Not least at the moment when they sat with lemonade under the shade of a tree and the conversation turned serious.

"What if I'm never fixed?"

"You're working hard," Cam reassured him. Because what else could he say? He had to believe that Gabriel would get to the point where he was able to move on from Stefan.

"I never told you what happened before Stefan," Gabriel said.

"I don't need to know," Cam said hurriedly. The last thing he wanted was for Gabriel to have to dig deep into his past when Cam was happy to wait.

Thing was, Cam really fucked up, because Gabriel stood up immediately, agitation in his voice, and anger. "Okay, I get it, you don't want to hear about the real me."

Cam heard him walk away, which was kind of shit, because he'd misunderstood Cam and also abandoned him under a tree somewhere.

"Gabriel!" he shouted. "Stop being an asshole! I meant I didn't need you to... Shit, come back and freaking listen to me."

"I'm here," a soft voice said right close to him. Seemed Gabriel hadn't walked that far.

Cam turned to the voice and held on to Gabriel's shirt. "I didn't mean anything wrong, or...hell, shit, I just meant that you'll tell me when you're ready, and if you feel like you can't talk now, you don't have to—not just for me."

"Yeah," Gabriel said sheepishly. "I was pushing you away. Clair explained that it's a coping mechanism. She even drew a picture in case I didn't get it. I like Clair; she listens to me. But I still have nightmares, Cam, about what led to me being on that street corner where Stefan found me."

Cam pulled him close and hugged him. Clearly talking was happening today. "I'm listening," he said.

"My mom was a housekeeper on this big ranch in Southern Texas, the Bar Five, and when she died they took me in. Or I guess I just got lost in the system somehow. I lived in this room over a barn, and I went to school for a while, and I never said anything. I don't know how they got away with it, but I know that slowly, as I got older, it was decided that horses were my thing, not book learning, so I stayed at the ranch. I didn't know any better, but one day it all changed."

Cam held Gabriel's hand, trying to be brave enough to listen to this, and inside he was scared to hear.

"There had been this young guy at the ranch, and he left, he got away, and I was next on Hank's radar, Hank being one of the brothers who owned and ran the Bar Five." He spoke so casually, but the words he used were choppy and harsh. "He was a fucking bastard; he got off on other people's pain. My pain. It wasn't just sex, but humiliation, and he would charge people for time with me."

Cam heard a sound—a low, keening groan—and realized it was him who'd let it out. Gabriel momentarily buried his face in Cam's neck, and Cam swore he could feel Gabriel's tears on his skin.

"One day, I ran. I don't know why I thought I'd get away—youthful optimism, I guess—only I didn't get far, and they broke my legs with baseball bats. It was…" He stopped talking, and now Cam was crying as well. "Horrible," Gabriel ended. How could he think of a word that would encompass everything he'd been through? Was there even a word that could describe that much evil?

"Then there was another boy, I don't know his name, but they killed him. Not outright—he hung himself. I stood in court, and I cried, and I told them everything, and Hank is in prison, and the Bar Five is gone."

"Jesus, Gabriel," Cam whispered, wiping at the tears that wouldn't stop. "You're so brave to have lived through that."

"And you can decide whether you need to step back,

and I wouldn't blame you. Clair explained that even the best of men could back away because they couldn't understand how I didn't fight back—"

Cam kissed him, a sloppy kiss with tears that was just off center, then toppled him to the ground, half lying on him and kissing him hard.

Gabriel tried to talk again, but Cam wouldn't let him, and they lay kissing under the tree until all the horrible words were lost in the kisses.

Cam felt powerless; he couldn't take away the memories, he couldn't save that ten-year-old boy, but he could love the man the boy had become.

And tell Gabriel that it mattered, that the things that had shaped him mattered, but that between them they could handle everything.

So that was what he did tell him, and Gabriel cried some more, but when they headed back to the ranch and Cam kissed Gabriel goodbye, the tension between them was different, easier.

"Text me," Gabriel demanded.

"Always," Cam answered, and shut the door. He wished he could watch Gabriel as they drove away, but worrying about not being able to see him was useless.

"Your dad called me to tell you to answer your damn phone, and he's at the hotel with Mitchell."

Cam smacked the back of his head against the headrest and cursed. Just what he needed.

The drive back to the hotel was quiet. Six didn't ask any questions or make comments, and Cam was fine with that. He had a lot to think about.

The meeting in his office was heated, Mitchell denying the reports that Cam had, implying that Cam didn't understand, and Sebastian defending his choice of Mitchell as both son-in-law and co-manager of the Dallas Royal. Cam let it all flow over him, listening to everything they had to say. Sebastian genuinely felt that Cam was overreacting. The only way he'd be able to get his dad to see anything would be for Sophie to be sitting there and telling her dad what Mitchell was really like.

"You've read the reports, Dad," Cam said for the third or fourth time. "I have several staff members accusing Mitchell of crowding them and touching them inappropriately."

No wonder victims didn't come forward when people like his dad refused to believe that kissing or prolonged, unwanted hugging was anything more than Mitchell playing around. The door opened, and he knew who it was before she said a single thing. Sophie. Six moved from the corner of the room, where he'd been waiting quietly. Cam relaxed, knowing that Six was looking out for Sophie.

"Mitchell," she said, so softly it made Cam's heart break. He swore if she showed any sign of going back to Mitchell, he would whisk her away to a desert island until she changed her mind.

"Sweetheart, I've been worried," Mitchell said. "I can't believe Cam has fed you all these lies—"

"Enough, Mitchell," Sophie said, her voice louder, more strident, with a thread of iron in it. "Daddy, Mitchell and I are getting a divorce," she announced.

There was a flurry of movement and a loud grunt.

"Stay right there," Six ordered, and Cam guessed he was saying that to Mitchell.

"I'm staying here in Dallas, right here with Cam, and I'm finishing my degree."

"And if she wants it, there's a role here in marketing," Cam said, abruptly convinced that was exactly what he wanted. The idea of having his sister close made him smile.

"There is?" she asked, then he could hear the smile in her voice. "You're on, Cam. I'll be citing Mitchell's unreasonable behavior and emotional abuse as grounds for divorce, if that's possible. He hurt me, he changed me, and I don't want him here."

Silence. Fuck, what was happening now? He gripped the desk when he sat down, suddenly furious that he could do nothing but sit there. And then his dad broke the silence.

"Six, escort Mitchell off the premises and call my lawyer."

Then Cam slipped from the room with Six. He didn't have to see to know that dad and daughter had a lot to discuss.

Visiting Legacy a few days later was the calm and peace to the chaos that had taken over his life. He'd grown used to the scents of horses and the ranch, and associated it all with Gabriel. Six wasn't staying today—this was a big celebration barbecue, and he'd organized a date with Clair, apparently—so Cam had decided to stay over. Picking up his overnight bag, he climbed down out of the cab and said his thank-yous and goodbyes even as Gabriel took his hand.

"This way," Gabriel said, and led him away from the SUV and over the bumpy ground to the ranch house, then along to where he knew Gabriel's room was. "See," he said triumphantly. Then, "My bad. I didn't mean see, because you can't… What I mean is, look, we have a… Shit. It's a bigger bed."

Cam couldn't help but tease. "Describe it for me," he said.

"Oh, it's a bed, with a mattress and…covers, they're pale blue…and… I don't know what else to say." He sounded adorably confused, and Cam couldn't help but pull him in for a kiss, which soon turned heated. Gabriel shut the door, and from the sound of it he locked it for good measure.

"Does it have four legs?" Cam deadpanned.

"What? Of course it— Wait… You're an asshole, Stafford," Gabriel said without heat.

"It sounds like a good bed," Cam began, letting out an unmanly squeak of surprise when Gabriel pushed him back onto the bed, then drew the blinds. Cam could hear them rattle as they fell. So if they were locked in, with no way of anyone seeing in, was this going to be the next step?

Cam gripped material and realized Gabriel was wearing a T-shirt, which he had up and over his head in an instant, running his hands over bare skin and letting out a hum of appreciation.

"Your turn," Gabriel said, and helped Cam to remove his shirt, and all the time he was talking. "I've been practicing, you know. I've been getting off and actually coming and everything in my head has been you. You holding me down and sucking me off, you fingering me…you want to do that? I've never done it for love before. I'm not sure it would make me come, but I could try."

They stripped off jeans and underwear until they were

nude and in a tangle of limbs. Gabriel was hard, Cam was harder, and they rubbed against each other, lost in a mess of kisses and whispered words. Cam swapped them so he was lying on top, kissing his way down Gabriel's chest, pausing at his navel and kiss-biting a trail to hip bones and down to his thighs, bypassing Gabriel's cock and hearing the mewl of disapproval.

"I want you to suck me," he said. "You need to get your mouth on me. I can move so that we could sixty-nine, then you could fuck me with your mouth."

Exasperated, Cam climbed back up Gabriel's body and kissed him hard. "Shhh," he whispered.

"What? You want me to talk dirty. You said you liked it, it got you off—"

Cam slapped a hand over Gabriel's mouth, gyrating his hips a little so their stiff cocks brushed against each other. "I need you to feel this for real," he said, with more kisses to Gabriel's throat. "Will you stop talking?"

Gabriel nodded, gripping Cam's ass tight and pushing up against him.

This was important; this was singularly the most vital sex that Cam would have in his life. This wasn't just sex, it was making love. He knew that, even if Gabriel didn't yet.

He moved his hand and kissed Gabriel hard, then felt Gabriel pushing something into his hand. "Lube," Gabriel murmured, "please... I've been practicing."

God, that was more arousing that all the porn talk Gabriel could ever use.

Cam slicked his fingers, slid down the bed a little and swallowed Gabriel down, then nearly choked when Gabriel sat upright in a flurry of motion. "We need to talk," he said.

Cam moved away a little, and Gabriel reached up to the shelf above the bed. "Condoms and a letter," he said. "I had tests. I'm okay, right, but I'm not ready to do this without you covering me." It sounded like that was a rehearsed line, and Cam couldn't have been prouder that Gabriel was taking control of his body and what he did and didn't want.

He wasn't sure he could fall more in love, but he did.

"I know you can't see them, but I can read them to you. I want to. You can trust me, I promise these are real."

Cam settled back on his knees. "Go on," he encouraged, because it was important to Gabriel.

Gabriel cleared his throat and proceeded to read the entire report from the heading to the footer. Then there was silence before the noise of rattling and tearing.

"It's on," Gabriel announced, then wriggled. Cam rested his hands on Gabriel, moving them to his thighs. Sex with Gabriel was going to be a hundred kinds of fun. "Sorry about the taste, but we could get some flavored ones if we do this again."

"If?" Cam said, and got back into the position he wanted to be in, locating the lube and squeezing it into his hand. He didn't care if it went everywhere; he wanted to feel Gabriel as he sucked him down, and he wanted to push inside.

Now who's thinking in porn terms?

He concentrated on the feel of Gabriel underneath the taste of the condom, and then he rubbed and sucked and pressed his cock against Gabriel's leg. It wasn't enough. He didn't want Gabriel coming in his mouth like this; he wanted to kiss him and tell him he loved him, and he released Gabriel's cock and kissed his way back up. He imagined Gabriel's expression. He'd been so close, and all it would take would be his fingers, the rhythm of their cocks rubbing against each other, and the kissing.

Oh god, the kissing.

"I'm coming," Gabriel said, his voice dripping with wonder.

"I love you," Cam said, his body tightening with the need to come, and then he felt Gabriel, the tension in his muscles, the exhalation of air, and there it was—Gabriel falling apart in his arms.

They hugged close, only moving when someone banged on the window and told them to break it up, which made them laugh but broke the incredibly intimate connection they had.

"One day, do you think you can love me?" Cam asked as they dressed. He was scared to hear the answer, unsure if Gabriel even thought he could ever love anyone. There was so much to fix, and so he thought the question should be out there, but it wasn't something he was expecting an answer to.

Gabriel sighed and wrapped his hands around Cam's waist. "I think I already do, but I have all this stuff in my head, about me, and how I see myself, and I want you to know I'd understand if you couldn't handle that."

Cam's chest tightened. "I'm not going anywhere."

Gabriel kissed him then. "It's when you say things like that I know I could be in love and really mean it."

"Then I want to say it again. Gabe, I love you."

"And I love it when you call me Gabe."

They laughed into the kiss. Everything would be okay.

"I need to ask you a huge favor. I have something I

need to do, and I need you to hold my hand when I do it."

"Okay." Cam didn't know what he was agreeing to, but he would do anything for Gabriel.

Dressed, they made their way outside, and the noise of a group of people grew larger as they walked along the uneven ground.

"Cam," a voice shouted, and he recognized it. Riley was there, which meant maybe Jack was, and the extended Double D ranch, kids, family, friends. Riley had talked at him for an hour about his family a couple of years back, about adoption and weddings and falling in love with Jack.

Everything had sounded so good. Sue him, but he'd craved that, even had a standing invitation to visit, but hell, how would he have fitted in?

"This way," Gabriel said, and tugged him away from Riley's voice. They passed by people who tried to say hello, but Gabriel didn't stop. Finally they came to a halt, and Gabriel's hold on his hand tightened.

"Darren?"

"Hey, Gabriel," a voice said.

"This is Cameron Stafford," Gabriel said. "Cameron, this is Darren, and his partner Vaughn."

Cam thrust out his free hand, and it was shaken twice.

Then Gabriel cleared his throat.

"Darren, this is for you." There was some movement as Gabriel passed something over.

"What is it?" Darren asked.

Vaughn chuckled. "He's giving you his dirty washing."

There was the sound of a zip, then a soft curse from Darren. "Shit, Gabriel, this is full of money, what the hell?"

"All of what I saved, except five hundred, which I will get to you as soon as I can. That is all the money you sent me from the sale of the Bar Five."

"That was for you."

"No," Gabriel said, cutting Darren off. "I don't want it. I want it to go to charity. I want you to choose."

"Okay, I can do that," Darren said. Clearly whatever expression Gabriel had going on was enough to make Darren think he should stop the debate right there.

There was a short silence, then it was Vaughn who spoke. "So you and Cameron here, then, you an item?"

"I'm working really hard on loving him," Gabriel announced.

And for want of something to say, Cam smiled and pulled Gabriel in for a kiss.

EPILOGUE

One year later

Gabriel reined Pixie to a stop, waiting for Cam to catch up. He was only now getting to be relaxed when he rode. At first he'd been terrified that the horse would just go wherever the hell it wanted if he didn't have any idea where to guide it.

So they'd given him Mistry, because she followed Pixie everywhere, and Cam couldn't go wrong with that.

"I swear this horse is playing with me," Cam groused as Mistry stopped right next to Pixie. "It felt like she was going in circles." He pushed his Stetson back, and Gabriel took a moment to admire the man he loved. Tonight, exactly one year since their first meeting in the elevator, Gabriel had things he wanted to say to Cam, and he wanted it to be out here, away from everyone and with the Texas soil beneath them.

"The sunset is amazing," he said. He'd got past the whole concept of not describing things in case it upset Cam. Particularly when Cam smacked him on the chest and told him in no uncertain terms that listening to Gabriel describe things was sexy. "It's fiery red and orange, and the ground is golden." He'd also become used to being super descriptive about what he could see. He never thought he'd use words like "vermillion" or "sensuous", but he damn well made sure to include them in sentences when he could.

Particularly when it ended up with Cam making love

to him.

This year had been long; the best and the worst. Stefan was dead. No one knew who, but they knew how. He'd been found with a needle in his arm, a huge overdose enough to have him gone. That had been a shock, a relief, a hell that he'd only just escaped from after all, who would they have pointed the finger at but him?

Six had made that accusation go away. Who knew how? He might be married to Clair, but that hadn't settled him down any—he was still edgy and dangerous.

Gabriel wasn't entirely convinced that Six hadn't had something to do with Stefan and the heroin, particularly after Stefan had appeared at the hotel demanding money in lieu of a tell-all exposé on the rich Stafford family and, in his words, their pet whore. Seemed like Six hadn't liked that.

"Sophie signed the papers today. Mitchell is out of her life," Cam said. "She told me to tell you that she wants to talk to you when you're next in town."

He didn't spend much time in the city, not quite ready to take that step to moving away from the ranch. But one day he and Cam would need a place to stay for good. Cam was relying more on a manager, and he and Sophie, who it seemed was getting quite cozy with said manager, spent a lot of time working from the ranch, mostly during the week, returning to the hotel on the weekends.

What they had wasn't conventional, but it was right.

"I'll come back with you this weekend," he said. "I know all she wants to do is hug me—she does that a lot."

"Who wouldn't want to hug you?" Cam said with a smile.

"There's a reason I brought you out here," Gabriel

began, and couldn't fail to notice the smile drop a little. Cam told him every day that he loved him. Never once did he falter, and not a single time did he expect an answer. Somehow the simple words had become something so much more than they should be.

Whereas with Cam they were an affirmation of how he felt, for Gabriel they would be an acceptance of himself, of forgiving the past, of knowing he had worth. Gabriel still feared rejection, and for the longest time he hadn't valued Cam's honesty and integrity. He had to face the wounds from his past, but he hadn't been ready to.

Those simple words were all big things to him. They meant everything.

"Is everything okay?" Cam asked, worried, his expression confused when Gabriel hadn't immediately started to talk.

Gabriel dismounted and helped to guide Cam down until they stood wrapped in each other's arms.

"I love you, Cameron Stafford," he said confidently. There was absolutely no way that Cam could fail to understand what this meant.

Cameron smiled at him, cradled his face like he had the first time they'd kissed, and then he closed his eyes like he always did.

"I love you," he said, and he kissed Gabriel.

And right there on the ridge overlooking Legacy Ranch, Gabriel made a promise to Cam in his heart, that he would always love him.

Because he and Cam were forever.

THE END

READ DANIEL'S STORY, IN THE THIRD LEGACY

Coming Spring 2018

A hidden past can only mean an uncertain future.

Daniel 'Danny' Flynn has made his way through college on an athletics scholarship. Danny had his hopes set on making the US Olympic team. When it looks like he may not make the cut, it seems his future is set in working with his aunt selling houses.

Corey Dryden is a journalist onto the story of the year. Four men, one abuser, and all connected to Dallas royalty—Jack and Riley Campbell-Hayes. Corey just needs a way in, and tracking down Daniel is his first step. This story could be award winning exposure for Corey's career, and he'll do anything to get what he needs. Can the lies he tells Danny lead to anything but heartbreak?

Because, Danny's past has to stay hidden, or it could destroy any hope of a future for either of them.

A new story set in the world of Jack and Riley Campbell-Hayes and the Double D Ranch, Texas.

* * * * *

Sign up for my newsletter for monthly updates, competitions, and news on releases.

READ JACK AND RILEY'S STORY IN THE TEXAS SERIES

The Heart of Texas

Riley Hayes, the playboy of the Hayes family, is a young man who seems to have it all: money, a career he loves, and his pick of beautiful women. His father, CEO of HayesOil, passes control of the corporation to his two sons; but a stipulation is attached to Riley's portion. Concerned about Riley's lack of maturity, his father requires that Riley *'marry and stay married for one year to someone he loves'.*

Angered by the requirement, Riley seeks a means of fulfilling his father's stipulation. Blackmailing Jack Campbell into marrying him "for love" suits Riley's purpose. There is no mention in his father's documents that the marriage had to be with a woman and Jack Campbell is the son of Riley Senior's arch rival. Win win.

Riley marries Jack and abruptly his entire world is turned inside out. Riley hadn't counted on the fact that Jack Campbell, quiet and unassuming rancher, is a force of nature in his own right.

This is a story of murder, deceit, the struggle for power, lust and love, the sprawling life of a rancher and the whirlwind existence of a playboy. But under and through it all, as Riley learns over the months, this is a tale about family and everything that that word means.

Books in the Texas Series

The Heart Of Texas
Texas Winter
Texas Heat
Texas Family
Texas Christmas
Texas Fall
Texas Wedding

For information on this series visit www.rjscott.co.uk

Made in the USA
Columbia, SC
22 March 2018